TRANSIT

GLOBAL AFRICAN VOICES

Dominic Thomas, editor

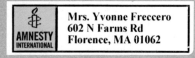

Abdourahman A. Waberi

TRANSIT

A NOVEL

TRANSLATED BY

DAVID BALL AND NICOLE BALL

Indiana University Press

BLOOMINGTON & INDIANAPOLIS

This book is a publication of

Indiana University Press
601 North Morton Street
Bloomington, Indiana
47404-3797 USA

iupress.indiana.edu

Telephone orders   800-842-6796
Fax orders   812-855-7931

© 2012 by Indiana University Press
© Editions GALLIMARD,
Paris, 2003

⊖ The paper used in this publication
meets the minimum requirements of
the American National Standard for
Information Sciences—Permanence
of Paper for Printed Library
Materials, ANSI Z39.48-1992.

Manufactured in the
United States of America

Library of Congress
Cataloging-in-Publication Data

Waberi, Abdourahman A., [date]
 [Transit. English]
 Transit : a novel / Abdourahman
A. Waberi ; translated by
David Ball and Nicole Ball.
 p. cm. — (Global African voices)
 ISBN 978-0-253-00683-7 (cloth
: alk. paper) — ISBN 978-0-253-
00689-9 (pbk. : alk. paper) — ISBN
978-0-253-00693-6 (e-Book)
 I. Ball, David, [date] II. Ball,
Nicole, [date] III. Title.
 PQ2683.A23T7313 2012
 843'.914—dc23   2012016244

1 2 3 4 5   17 16 15 14 13 12

Cover illustration: Sunset behind the mountains near Djibouti.
Photo by Guenter Guni.

To Émile Olivier,

*To my mother and my brother Ahmed
and to Lucien and Azeb Roux,
Jean-Dominique Penel,
and Ali Coubba,*

AS A TOKEN OF FRIENDSHIP

Thank you, my land; for your remotest
Most cruel mist my thanks are due,
By you possessed, by you unnoticed,
Unto myself I speak of you.
And in these talks between somnambules
My inmost being hardly knows
If it's my demency that rambles
Or your own melody that grows.

—VLADIMIR NABOKOV

From *The Gift*, translated from the Russian by
Michael Scammell with the collaboration of the
author (New York: G. P. Putnam's Sons, 1963), p. 68.

Contents

Preface

Transit is as fresh and relevant today as when it first appeared in France in 2003. This is a terrible—and wonderful—thing to say.

Terrible, because its picture of an impoverished country ravaged by war and repression is still the reality of life in Djibouti, that little country squeezed between Somalia, Ethiopia, and Eritrea at the edge of the Horn of Africa. The drought that devastated these countries was not the only cause of the famine that reached catastrophic proportions in 2011; it merely aggravated the conditions we see through the eyes of the characters of *Transit,* even if those characters were created nearly a decade ago. Terrible, too, because its portrayal of their desperate attempt to flee the country is still relevant today—and not only in Djibouti.

But the freshness and relevance of *Transit* is also wonderful, as Waberi's creations live in our minds the way characters in real works of literature do. The chapters in *Transit* are a succession of monologues by each of the characters in the novel: Bashir, a very young veteran of Djibouti's civil war; Harbi, a Djiboutian intellectual and an opponent of the regime; Harbi's

French wife, Alice, and their son, Abdo-Julien; and Abdo-Julien's grandfather Awaleh. Their interlocking voices, by turns poetic and critical, tell their stories and the story of their country, giving us Djibouti's history, politics, and physical, economic, and moral landscape in their own language, their own style. All of them propel the action toward its end—an end fraught with political meaning.

One character gives us the same kind of pleasure we have in reading great tragicomic works of literature: Bashir, the poor, adolescent ex-soldier. His monologues are delivered in a slangy, comical language very much his own, a mix of naïveté and sly, often cynical, observation. He's the one who reveals the real condition of the country and all the horrors perpetrated during the civil war and after—child soldiers, arms trafficking, drugs (the ever-present khat and "pink pills"), random killing, hunger—and exposes France, the former colonial power, as a hypocritical arbiter between the warring camps.

As translators, we must say Bashir gave us a hard time. How to turn into English Waberi's invention of a spicy, lower-class, "incorrect" French spoken by a shrewd but uneducated boy? Our admiration for Waberi's creation was mixed with anxiety. The worst thing one could do, we felt, would be to flatten him into ordinary normative English: the character would simply disappear. On the other hand, we didn't want him to sound like one of the ghetto characters in the HBO series *The Wire:* he's not an African American kid from the projects but an adolescent from Djibouti. And somehow, he should sound like that in English. The author suggested we turn to Ken Saro-Wiwa's *Sozaboy,* another first-person narrative of civil war in Africa, and that did help in a number of ways. First, *Sozaboy* gave us a model of "incorrect" African English ("A Novel in Rotten English" is its subtitle), which, like Bashir's French, seems spoken rather than written. (But here, too, we had to be careful; unlike

Saro-Wiwa's narrator, Bashir is not a Nigerian, and there's no reason why he should sound like one.) And then, we could see how Waberi was inspired by that magnificent novel: in *Sozaboy* too, the horrors of war and the abuses of power are related with great simplicity by a very young man. Comparing the two works increased our appreciation of the essentially comic nature of Waberi's invention, however dark the comedy may be. Saro-Wiwa's *Sozaboy* is, finally, a harrowing and depressing novel; Waberi's *Transit* has something almost upbeat about it—above all, paradoxically, Bashir's account of murder and mayhem. His satiric relation of the recent history of the Horn of Africa and his quick portraits of Djiboutian political leaders are often quite funny: the use of the faux-naïf to deflate political pretense is a tried and true satiric technique, and Waberi does it well. We can only hope that we did him justice when we brought Bashir's voice into English.

Not everything in the literary universe of *Transit* is dark comedy, far from it. The voices of other characters are often lyrical, and here, too, we can only hope that we were able to render that very different tone in English. The novel also presented us with bitter evocations of Djibouti's colonial past and sometimes nostalgic evocations of the nomadic past and the customs of its people, themes that appear again and again in the author's work.

It is worth noting that Waberi gave his collection of poems a title that might be translated as *The Nomads, My Brothers, Go Out to Drink from the Big Dipper (Les Nomades, mes frères, vont boire à la Grande Ourse)*. This element of the traditional life of the region is transmitted through the grandfather, Awaleh. Under different names, the grandfather figure, a transmitter of tradition, appears as a recurrent figure in Waberi's work. He is a teller of tales. A former nomad, Awaleh deplores colonization and progress, both of which have led to the loss of cultural and tribal identity. "Luckily I'm here to connect the threads of spiritual and temporal things, the visible and the invisible," he says. He is a pious, tolerant Muslim. In one poetic chapter addressed to his grandson, he celebrates the nomads and their resistance to the colonial administration. In another particularly eloquent chapter, he describes scenes of famine (and takes a dim view of international aid organizations). One of his favorite interlocutors is Harbi's French wife, Alice. She and their son, Abdo-Julien, transmit through their discourse—and their very existence—other themes and ideals dear to Waberi's heart: multiculturalism, tolerance, and *métissage*.

Two of the main characters (Harbi and Bashir) are speaking from the Roissy airport. The overarching structure of *Transit*, and the connection between Bashir and Harbi, is only revealed in Bashir's last monologue, although there are hints of it earlier. The structure is a cleverly devised loop, as the reader will discover. After Bashir's last monologue, at the very end of the novel, we find a poetic epilogue that takes us back to the prologue: Harbi, speaking for all the exiles on our planet, is in the airport of Roissy–Charles de Gaulle, waiting—waiting to enter France, like Bashir, where they will live the lonely, miserable life of most refugees, as we sense from what Harbi has already told us about his fellow exiles. We have come full circle.

Abdourahman A. Waberi was born in 1965 in what was then French Somaliland (the French gave it another name in 1967); it became Djibouti when it gained its independence in 1977. In 1985, Waberi won a scholarship to study in France. He lived, studied, and worked there until 2009, when he became a Fellow in the Humanities at Wellesley College and then accepted a position at the Claremont Colleges in California, where he currently teaches. He spends his time between the United States and France and remains a nomad at heart, as he likes to say: he travels widely, and Africa is often one of his destinations. He has written four novels, three books of short fiction, a book of poems, and numerous articles and essays. Waberi is one of the leading francophone writers of his generation, internationally recognized, one of those to whom the French novelist J. M. G. Le Clézio dedicated his Nobel Prize for Literature in his acceptance speech. Translated into over half a dozen languages, Waberi's work explores the themes of migration, colonial and postcolonial suffering, and resistance with great linguistic invention and originality.

Waberi has won many literary prizes and honors in France, Germany, and elsewhere. His satiric *In the United States of Africa* (in which Africa is rich and bloated, while the wretched of the earth live in war-torn Euramerica and desperately try to immigrate to a united Africa) appeared here in 2009; he received lavish praise from the major literary journals in France for his latest novel, published in 2011, *Passage des larmes* (*Passage of Tears*), a grim dialogue of the deaf between two brothers in Djibouti, a fanatical Islamist and a North American exile who works for a private international intelligence agency. We are delighted that Indiana University Press is now publishing his second novel, *Transit*, one of Waberi's most important works.

David Ball
Nicole Ball

PROLOGUE

Never again will a single story be told
as though it's the only one.

—JOHN BERGER

BASHIR

I'M IN PARIS, *warya**—pretty good, huh? OK it's not really
Paris yet but Roissy. That the name of the airoport. This airoport got two names, Roissy and Charles de Gaulle. In Djibouti
it got just one name, Ambouli, an I swear on the head of my
departed family, it's much-much tinier. OK, this trip here, everything went all right. I gobbled the good food of Air France.
Went direct to the war film before I fell into heavy sleep. I was
stocked, no I mean scotched—taped—in the last row of the
Boeing 747 where the cops tie the deportees up tight when the
plane goes back to Africa. That's true, that the way they do it.
Moussa he told me that a little while ago. Moussa, you know he
can pray the good Lord sitting down without lifting his behind
from the seat of the plane, believe me faithfully. He travel a lot,
Moussa, helps guys discovering travel like me. He calm all the
time. He talk so soft-soft you'd think he got sore tonsils. Wait,
I'm gonna follow Moussa, pick up baggage. My bag blocked between two big boxes of French military, label says it: "AD 188," I
know what that is, it Air Detachment 188, navigation base right

next to airoport in Ambouli as a matter of fact. I pulled the bag hard. A white lady looked at me, you know, with her eyes in the air like white marbles. I picked the bag up hard like we did with our gear when I was mobilized in the army. I put my bag on my back. I looked right-lef. I see Moussa, I walk behind him. Act dumb with the cops, Moussa he confirm it to me. Main thing, don't show you speak French. Don't mess things up, so shut your trap. Or cry, to fish pity from French people. French in France nicer than French back there, Moussa don't say that, I know by myself. I stocked the esperience. ok I don't say nothing cause Roissy's danger, they might say Africans, pains in the ass. I look right-lef again, I walk behind big Moussa. Shut up. Nod head yes, shake head no, and that's it, ok? Shut trap, waggle head, or cry a lot to fish pity. That's it. Period. I walk forward a little, follow Moussa.

Oh yah—I dropped my real name, Bashir Assoweh. For six months now my name been Binladen, Moussa he choked on his coffee in plastic cup they give you. *Never* say that again here he say. That get the French fierce, and the English, and the Americans, and even the nice Norwegians who pay the ngos for us and keep their traps shut. But me, I like that, you say Binladen and everybody drop dead with panic like I'm real kamikaze they stop in front of barbwire and sambags of the American Embassy in Djibouti. Binladen, dunno who he was before but anyways he look great. Bushy white beard with black thread, white horse not like the gray camel of our Bedouins and specially that Kalashnikov on his shoulder. His beard real-real nice but hey he not really prophet cause true prophet has no photo. In Djibouti, they said, yell "Long live Binladen" everywhere, that's how I know his name, then stop right away or else it Gabode prison for everybody, mamas, uncles, kids, everybody. But that still secret. I didn't say a thing, right? Djibouti over, Roissy here, gotta watch out saying anything come into my head.

HARBI

ROISSY. Air France. Daily flight to Saint-Denis de la Réunion via Cairo and Djibouti. The overbooked, overwhelmed airline is transferring some of its passengers to other airlines like Air Afrique. People willing to switch can make up to a thousand francs on the deal. OK? OK! You did the right thing. New situation. The line there is ten times longer. A mountain of luggage. Huge crowd. Everybody chewing gum with great energy. I spot Kaba Something-or-other, a guy with the look of a Sahelian Mafioso; he's knocking the whole line about with his cumbersome bags and wants to charm me into giving him a hand. Boarding time for the Africans being deported "of their own free will." A dozen or so scheduled to be transported the usual way; three male individuals will be locked up in the cramped space of the restrooms, piled in and immediately incarcerated quick as two whiffs of a cigarette. A man wearing a glaring yellow vest with the word "technician" on his back, helped by three PAF[1] agents, has stuck a thick roll of gray tape on the restroom door so the passengers who happen to have missed the caging or whose

1. Police de l'Air et des Frontières.—*Author's note*

5

eyes had avoided it won't venture into those restrooms. Strange how the same scene keeps being repeated almost every day on other flights always bound for some African destination. Each time, the unfortunate deportee tries squealing like a tortured whale just to stir the conscience of the ordinary passenger, usually a tourist. Today's deportee is Congolese, supposedly a shopkeeper from Pointe Noire, and his fate seems sealed. A few moments later on the Airbus, there are some angry reactions among the passengers, followed by a nauseous feeling culminating in a widespread urge to throw up. And considering the passenger's extreme state of agitation, the captain finally gives in after some heated negotiations and the troublemaker is taken off board, returned to his cell, and put back into the retention center in a waiting zone of the airport. At least he's alive, luckier than the ones who die of dehydration in the Arizona desert or freeze to death inside the undercarriage of some cargo plane.

I'm alone now, alone without Alice, my dear wife, without Abdo-Julien, our only child, without my father, Awaleh, who used to travel along with us in spirit. Lost in the bowels of Roissy airport. I went through them often when I was a student, or on business trips or, more frequently, when visiting Brittany. I have an old debt of memory to settle with France; people think migrants arrive naked in a new land at the end of their odyssey; yet migrants are loaded with their personal stories and heavier still with what is called collective history.

That shrinking land of ours is crisscrossed with people in perpetual motion. Not a week goes by without some African team back from a sporting competition unanimously asking for political asylum in Frankfurt, Athens, or Glasgow. There are glorious sunrises, happy times ahead, bursts of light that turn, alas, into water and mud. Happiness? Don't make me laugh! It all makes me dizzy. For now, I'm going to take a rest. It's like the silence of the desert here; the hours go by in neutral. Nothing to do except think, rehash the past, obsess over it endlessly, come up with projects that may or may not see the light of day, not to mention that little voice whispering you have no right to forget the ones who're still in jail, how can you drag your body around without feeling guilty? I left my heart at home, I only have my body to care for now, and for that, I'll have to find some good soul to help me apply for political asylum and guide me through the bureaucratic labyrinth, like that damn OFPRA,[2] the open sesame for any aspiring candidate for exile. For a long time now, I've accepted the idea that I'm going to die like everyone else and I'm not about to change my mind. I cannot wait to find peace of mind and body again. To tame my mind where morbid, incongruous ideas keep running wild, and snuff out that snickering little voice. Glue the pieces of my dislocated being back together. In short, get used to my new identity. A memory anchored deep in the nest of my brain is coming back to me. I must have been a child of four or five then, and I can recall the frightened look in my eyes very clearly. One day, as I was walking with my aunt along one of the avenues in our neighborhood, I passed by a military patrol. Like a chrysalis about to burst, the question popped out instantly:

"Who are those people?"

"The French, our colonizers."

"Why are they here?"

"Because they're stronger than we are."

My country was born more than two decades ago, wrapped in the flag designed by Mahmoud Harbi.[3] I was young, handsome, and strong. I'd been back home for three years, equipped with a big diploma, big for that time at any rate, and accompanied by a young, touching, stubborn woman I'd met when I was a stu-

---

2. Office de Protection des Réfugiés et Apatrides.—*Author's note*
3. An important figure in Djiboutian resistance to colonization.—*Author's note*

dent in France. In 1977, Djibouti was stepping down from the high solitude of being the last colonial stronghold. My country was brought into the world wrapped in its flag (blue, green, white, and red star), and I was in my prime, hardly thirty.

1

BASHIR BINLADEN

I WAS BORN YESTERDAY, I'm just saying, I mean I was born
not so long ago, and even for this little chick of a country I'm
not too-too over the hill, see. We're the same age, this coun-
try-here and myself, so believe me faithfully I snoop and look
everywhere, men an animals like fine clean dressed-up dogs,
stuff natural like women's thing. Rocks an flowers too. Oh
Lord, I kind of lost Moussa an I got so-so scared. I'm talking
all alone to buck myself up, I look overhere or overthere and I
can't see nothing... I'm at Roissy, in front of the paradise of the
Whites, gotta keep cool, act like professional military. I stare
everywhere and name everything I see in the rush an crush of
voices an lives. I do love sniffing out people; gotta sniff em up,
sort of like them clean well-groomed dogs. That way you avoid
problems an bullshit, little sonsabitches think they're Tintin's
Captain Haddock. I hate soft old chewngums with no taste. I'm
not afraid of nothing, not even foreigners (oh no! am I off my
rocker or what? the foreigners, that's us now, the natives here,
it's them). That's what we learned in the school of the streets
cause real school way-way past. First I was born in tiny little
village, Damerjogh its name. After that we came to the big city

for my daddy's job. For he always like that, always at port being that longshoreman-there. So me, I cut out quick into the street, to look an look, an learn real-real good. School wasn't my thing, sure I finished fourth grade like everybody else, but school-there back home it's total pyramid. If you lucky you get big diploma, or else it's the street for you, like me. When I finish fourth grade they tell me fit for active work (we call that AW, active work). What you gonna work, little like that? So my whole neighborhood AW. After AW, I did everything in street. That's what I did to get by. Today my mom an dad not around no more to esplain me things I can't understand. I'm not so lucky, I'm all alone with no brother or sister in a country where every family can be a soccer team all by itself or send an emergency brigade straight to planets like Startrek.

Before, there was war back home, the war kind of over now cause the Big Foreigners they say: better stop that war right away or no foreign aid. The president he said OK before anybody else. Open little parenthesis. If I was president of the country of course I'd change my name. I'd call myself *Moi* like the president of that Kenya-there. *Moi*, it's best president name I know. *Moi*, it simple—beautiful too, right? OK, close parenthesis. So the ministers who wanted to go on with war were pushed out of the offices. The president signed peace with first group of rebels, Frud 1 it's called. Today two years after the war, we're up to Frud 4 (Front for the Restoration of Unity and Democracy, it said that on the big sign in front of Palace of the People). Restoration is very correct word too, they even say that in real French from France. Politicians, they never stop eating, stuffing their face, gobbling, suffocating on the leftovers. Fill belly fat as Port container. I'm saying Port cause Port's just across the way. People who know that, they not gonna say Binladen's a lie an a liar. After the war, end of the line, Sergeant Houmed yelled every day. We demobilized. You can leave this minute if you want. War's over. They gave us demobilize soldiers 40,000 DF and it's bye-bye front, gunpowder, an thirst. So I gave a lot-lot to the family an the tribe. The cousins who been unemployed ever since they could stand, they party with my money. A weeklong bash, two thousand francs a day, what with the khat, the girls, the taxi I paid for with a girl once cause I was being class, man. I was still wearing my American jeans an my wide belt I kept. We all kept a little something from the army. And anyways OK, war over. Ayanleh, he still wear his big army shoes. Aïdid, he walk around with his commando helmet on his head. Warya, they say that rifle he hid, he sold it to a jealous husband to rip the heart of the guy always after Naya, his honey who bleach her skin. Naya, she so-so strong for love. She volcano-love her honey says.

Oh, the army was big mess. Holy moley! We killed the Wadags, screwed their daughters, poisoned wells all the way to Moussa Ali, you don't know Moussa Ali, it's border. After that it's Eritrea, careful, don't mess around with Eritrea like our president doing now cause Eritrea stronger than Zidane for war. It's Ronaldo the Brazilian. They fucked Mengistu an all the Ethiopians with fifty times more harms than them. Ethiopians they got so much harms, right after Chinese, Japanese, Hindis, and so on–so on. So, Wadags they wanted peace right away. Pretty natural—they don't all wanna die. Frud 1, Frud 2, Frud 3, Frud 4, all the same and one. Lotta bullshit, yah. From now on, just to kid around we call that Frud-there Scud like Iraqi missile not always effective. Restoration, OK, that's good. Democracy, that hotair of politicians who take bread from whoever giving it.

After the war, for a few weeks it was a free-for-all. We did whatever we wanted. Ate in restaurants without paying, pirated big Arab and Hindi shopkeepers, even small shopkeep-

ers native like us. Grabbing merchandise quick as chameleon
gobbling flies. Even from mamas selling vegetables an khat on
Place Rambo. When I say "Place Rambo" it's funny, sounds like
real French name Rimbaud, right? Reminds me of singing in
school *Alaclairefontainééé, menononproméné, jaitrouvélosiclair
quéjémisuisbaiyé...* "Attaclearfountain, zahwenwokin, ahfoun-
wattasocleah ahswimnit." After the war, we did whatever we
wanted. Beat up on people in the street for fun, robbed Arab
and Hindi hardware stores. Drilled girls day an night. Goverment don't say nothing. There's still chaos, the situation will
soon return to normal, said Morning Hyena, Minister of Police,
on DRT. DRT, you don't know what that is yet, right? Djibouti
Radio Television, it's written in big gold letters on the building,
next to the Presidential. The asshole general who screwed up
his military coup so bad, well, he got all his men together at the
DRT. Thinks coup mean only TV, radio—DRT, see? The loyola
tanks—or whatever, I forgot the word—anyway president's
tanks they left from Camp Sheikh-Osman, went through all
of Ambouli. Went through the traffic circle that go into Port
road. Then, they go behind Arhiba and the asshole general's
base right next to it. They don't shell police base of the asshole
general. They come straight to DRT. Fourteen rounds of mortars, bang, bang, bang, the coup guys they sure cried loud for
their mamas. Twelve down. The troublemakers, quick-quick
prisoners without they hurt a goverment fly. The asshole general he left to hide in the French naval base, on the Plateau
du Héron. The president came quick-quick out of his hiding
place in Sheikh-Osman military camp, the one the asshole general spared. He get his troops together. I have triumphed he
yell loud-loud. They all on TV a couple hours later. Morning
Hyena, Stuffed Hyena, Pushy Hyena, Toothless Lion, etc., all
there. Still shaking with fear. You could see the sweat flood-
ing their faces on the color screen TV. Then, the president left

with head of diplomacy to get the asshole general that used to be his true-true friend before, when they making restoration together. Together they knew how to conjugate the verb have, not the verb to be.

What do you think the French did with the president's request and the so-rich words of the head of diplomacy? I say request, that a very correct word, they say it on black-an-white TV even, like at Samireh's our neighbor the shopkeeper. The French they say we are presently handing over the general (only they don't add asshole, like me, Binladen) if you in Djibouti respect the rightsaman too like in our country. The general has the right to be assisted by the lawyer of his choice before he even opens his mouth. He has right to a fair trial, insisted the ambassador in a shirt with red-white-an-blue flowers before presently handing over the asshole general. President happy as a clam, he busted the asshole general. Hey, he together again with his lieutenants in the terriblific Gabode prison. The motherfucka now with the little Ethiopian thieves he used to bust himself, I say little cause the big ones they still out there, making restoration with the president's wife.

Worst off in this whole business is regular little soldiers, that's what City say. I don't agree. Little soldiers, they used to be little darlins of the asshole general (no way he deserves a capital G), they did anything they wanted, selling off gas ration coupons, stealing the refugees' bags of food, borrowing people's cells, drilling girls—even the girls of their neighborhood got diarrhea when they saw them. Besides, little soldiers, sure thing! They're all sergeants, second lieutenants, lieutenants. No ordinary draftee like us in their department. There's even a colonel, I obliterated his name—I like to use big fancy words like the French, in my own personal language. City a hypocrite, double hypocrite. They forget to say people-there all cousins of the tribe, so same cousins same aunt same uncle, I say. And tomorrow if the president fired the asshole general City would say so-so unfair etcetera etcet. Me I'm telling you City don't know what they want. One day they cheering real loud for the president specially when a boat comes into our port with li-quidities (yes, liquidities the word, in fact very correct word). Next day, they say: we support the opposition. Our bold, active opponent, the Pele of the opposition, he was journalist an sol-dier before, so, he sick of City, believe me faithfully. He better off leaving for France like me Binladen, like all the others I see here at Roissy hugging the walls, like the intellectual genle-man who lost his French wife and his rich-kid son. Matter of fact, president will get out too, when there nothing left to eat. Restoration over. That man-there, he like ole empty battery can't start up the country no more. So, everybody's salary ten months overdue. Not one head of a boat in port, not one tail of a plane stopped over with white tourists saying Reunion, Mauritius, Malagascar, wow! it's too-too hot. And the stupid idiots come to Djibouti for a breath of fresh air!

Now I'm gonna show you the poem Monsieur Djama our principal recited to us in elementary school of District 6. That's where I live in Djibouti, actually. My buddy Ayanleh found it in his small little brother's things. Monsieur Djama, he's a funny one. He been giving same poem to all his pupils for ten year or what? I don't get all of it, no big deal, right? I'm gonna show it to Moussa who's coming back loaded like a Yemenite donkey (donkey rub donkey, that a naughty proverb of ours). Yemenites strong for business, Yemenites king of commerce right after Hindis who sad like a day without khat. Hey, Moussa gonna read it to you:

> In Djibouti it's so hot,
> Metallic, bitter, brutal,
> They grow palm trees of metal
> The others die on the spot.

You sit beneath the scrap iron
While, grinding in the desert breeze
They pile up to your very knees,
the iron filings.

But under palms that sound like trains
Luckily, inside your brain
You're free to fantasize
A trip worldwide.

OK poetry fine but hey, what I wanna do is tell you more about my life. I can tell you right away I never got one slap in the face from my daddy. Papa he wasn't very old when he died, too-too broke down by his longshoreman job, but gentle like little lamb fresh from its mama's belly. He'd piss blood like that for no reason before he checked out. Me, I'm still running. When I was a baby I was already running a lot-lot. I also liked the games kids play like soccer. Not so many soccer games around no more. The city going through a difficult period, maybe Papa could've esplained you the how and why of all the problems. Veterans, the handicapped an disabled from civil war, they all demonstrate yesterday front of Presidential Palace (*beit al wali** the old folks say, that Arabic) asking for their puny pensions not paid for months. Hey, what you think goverment did? They fired on the crowd of cripples, with real bullets. A lot of corpses, lot of wounded on the boulevard to presidential palace. An guess what, no one lifted a finger. The crowd run away like scared little chicken. The wounded more or less taken care of and the dead buried in dead bush silence.

Same evening, City clapped regular as a broken toilet at the president's endless speech. So's not to think of their pain, everybody get giddy on rumors. They go like this: yah-yah we gonna get revenge this time, yah, arright. . . . Our bellies grumbling with the noise of rising waters, the noise of a fast-moving stream over stones. Like we're wolfing down the bitter mango, bitter mango even ants and little insects won't eat it.

2

ABDO-JULIEN

AS A CHILD I walked around naked every blessed day. My protruding belly button would catch the eye like a smiling little sun. A sun the color of licorice at night, copper-color in the afternoon. My mom was entirely devoted to me. I was her first sun, her only sun to this very day. Maman kept repeating to whoever would listen that this country was hers too. This is where love made me put down my bags, she would say. It's a five-camel hotel, she'd repeat without really realizing how ridiculous the image sounded. Everything in this land is mine: its volcanic hillocks, its skinny fauna; the tragic, camel-like swaying of its hips; the aquatic flora pictured on postage stamps; the desert islets like the famous Guinni Koma (also called l'île du Diable, Devil's Island by the French). I can feel its salt on my body. I am this pit like a wounded vulva between the hills. You'd think she was reading from a geography textbook. Yes, everything here is mine. The salt lakes, the bald peaks, the whimsical firmament at Lake Assal, the small forest from times long past, the limestone high plateaus, the Grand Bara and Petit Bara, the main summit culminating at almost seven thousand feet. The bitter waters and their extraordinary salinity. The liquid heart of the gulf, its solitude crenellated with waves. Her world forever inviolable. This is my country stirring the air just like the lyre palm and the traveler tree dragging its exiles over the crust of the earth. My country running breathlessly, endlessly. My country sad and beautiful like the oilcloth of a village café in Brittany on a rainy Sunday morning. My dad and I would burst out laughing. She's stubborn and endearing. And there she goes now, changing the subject and the textbook. From geography to history. My country's history in the annals of the continent? Barely room for a lowly footnote at the bottom of a page. Seventy thousand square miles of hatred and misery, my country of ergs and acacias. She's flying off the handle now, excited as a young goat.

Choice? Do you really think you can choose your destiny in life? Only morons or gullible fools believe such nonsense. It's true that I wanted wind in my sails, light in my eyes, a child in my womb, a black member in the hollow of my belly, and what else? My chest chock-full of air. Chastity, poverty, and obedience are not my most cherished vows. I'm not a chick raised in a poultry factory. But before meeting some spindly students on a college campus in Rennes, how was I supposed to know I would land in Djibouti and forever leave the house with its walls eaten away by the black grape vine? Choice? Don't make me laugh. What on earth made me go there, in the midst of those strange strangers with their Afros and bell-bottom pants? You always like to think of yourself as different; you want to escape the common fate, out of pride perhaps. To speed up the end of adolescence. What am I doing here? I let myself be sucked up by destiny, something stronger than myself, like the current of the tide that carries away the careless swimmer. Why would a young student, a girl from Brittany like me, set out for this crazy place? Fate took over and I dove into it headfirst. Jesus, that feeling of having bought a one-way long-distance ticket!

They seemed lost; so was I but a lot less than they were. They looked gentle, sweet, harmless. So did I, they said, afterwards. I knew nothing about them, about their country, their language, their culture. I had just turned twenty; I was just coming out of the awkward teens. Life was ahead of me; it was possible to change it, as we kept saying at the time, a time that seems today almost as remote as geological eras. And with one snap of the fingers, everything picked up speed; everything became clear. It's not the word "passion" that came to mind when I started to be around them a bit—of course not. It was the word "puzzlement" at first. They were always in groups, as if they were on duty together. They did everything together, in packs almost, like the ants in the documentaries they show on French TV late into the night. This compact conglomerate was very strange to me at the beginning. Then I got used to their gregarious ways, their nomadic flesh that would start moving only as a group, with their worries locked inside themselves more often than not. They'd laugh and joke in rhythm; they're sure good at that, bigger jokers you won't find. I was friendly with all of them, laughing with one, laughing with all. Since no one could muster enough courage to pick me up, it took a long time before I could be all alone with your father, discover pleasure with him—the kind you call carnal—and before we could thrill together. He seemed unhappy to leave his gang just to spend an afternoon at the movies with me, but proud as a peacock as I was, I would never allow myself to rein him in. So he would make a date with me and then cancel at the last minute, saying he had forgotten his Interafrican soccer game. It was trendy at the time to form teams by countries and fight on the soccer field. A lot better than the meetings of cabinet ministers in the OAU,[1] as the jolly Dieudonné, the fast center forward from Togo, would

1. Organization of African Unity.—*Author's note*

say jokingly. Dieudonné Gnammanckou, what kind of a name is that, a guy from Morocco would grumble—always the same guy, the one with a chip on his shoulder, but he could run faster than Jesse Owens and he was generous with his passes on the field. My God, your father made me watch so many of those damn games! Him and me, we could talk and understand each other in a split second, a split word, a split smile. Making love with him was easy as having a glass of water. And believe me, my foggy Brittany hadn't prepared me for that. With him, I was always stewing in cayenne pepper. When I think about it now I tell myself I was being buoyed up in an ocean of tales without beginning or end. I know what I mean. If going so far away, into such a far-off elsewhere, didn't bother me, it's because nostalgia and its double, melancholia, are quite foreign to my nature.

Of Brittany, I miss nothing. Not the sugared crepes or the crepes flambé in *chouchen* cider, nor the liquid skies and the rain-wind of Mont-Saint-Michel, nor the vacations at Saint-Pierre-de-Quiberon (they were from the land on my father's side, from the sea on my mother's, and that's why schooners, longshoremen and their strikes, deep-sea fishing, foggy docks, caravels, puffins, pelicans, chebecs and clippers, trawlers, seaweed and seafarers, frigates, the navy, overcast skies, the Azorean anticyclone, the waters of the Gulf of Gascony, Ouessant, and Roscoff, Aix and Oleron, the beaches of Finistère and even far-off Cape Horn were all part of family conversation), the noisy folklore in Lorient or Morlaix in the summertime, with its sprightly carousels of boozers and bagpipe blowers. I have no need for memory, that cumbersome totem. No Proustian remembrance of things lost for me, no madeleines, no little patch of yellow wall. And I might as well tell you right now: Celtic music really gets on my nerves. I can't retrieve that memory unless I'm under hypnosis. It's epidermal, it's contagious, that's all. End of story.

Sometime before her tragic death, she confided to me that when she was a teenager, her nose was a little too hooked. One of those little defects nature bestows on you for life. As you might guess, that made her self-conscious, and her family never failed to remind her of it. They had decided that she should have her nose fixed. She was shaking with fear, fear of dying, fear of not waking up, fear of sinking into the arms of her anesthesiologist for good. Her legs, soft as cotton, couldn't carry her any longer. An appointment had been scheduled shortly before summer. The date was nearing. They kept coddling her, reassuring her as best they could. But her fear only intensified. And yet, a miracle happened. It came from the clinic of Doctor Lucien Roussel, the most famous plastic surgeon in Brittany. He's the one who put an end to that panic fear. Three days before she was due for surgery, he committed suicide.

In the history books, articles, and newspaper clippings Maman used for her research, bringing them back from the National Archives of Overseas Territories in Aix-en-Provence, you find numerous terms and insulting denominations, the wild theories of anthropologists or preposterous tribologists that should be stowed away deep inside the warehouse where historical anathemas are stored and forgotten. Not to mention, Papa would say, that school of tropical geography that never got out of the claws of the colonial lobby. They're a real pain in the neck (let me tell you, I'd just as soon get smacked in the kisser by a shepherd's stick, Maman would say if she heard me talk like a little professor) with their poor little men oppressed by their climate, their volatile acacias married to the desert winds, technically deprived, threatened by pandemics, bedimmed by sleeping sickness, reduced to living naked, and overwhelmed by a soaring birthrate. They keep talking about those minds filled with wonder and innocence, fed by the milk of France, their savior and benefactor. In the editorials of the time, we were always subjected to the risks of mutilating choices: convert or exploit them, educate or emasculate them, develop or crush them. "Exterminate all the brutes!" vociferated Conrad's counterpart, someone who knew how to speak the language of truth. As a young thirty-two-year-old sailor, he had commanded a steamer that went up the Congo River in 1890. *Heart of Darkness* is simply the fictitious version of his logbook, and Kurtz is only applying the techniques then in use to exploit gold, ivory, and wood on the property of good old king Leopold of Belgium.

I have ungrudgingly revealed to you my intuitions and the kind of books I read. It's up to you to finish the job, if you feel like it. I'll even help with the bibliography if need be. And if I were you, I wouldn't stop here.

Maman's eyes are blue, Papa's are black, mine are brown. Maman, she's grace itself and Papa—forget it! My eyes? Brown, and light, she often adds. Moumina (Memona, that's how my funny half-Breton mom pronounces it), the girl who works for us, has gray eyes like a cat, which has oblong pupils, as you well know. She also has two high round breasts, what am I saying, she has two ogival arches thrusting upwards into the sky, an aquiline nose close to my heart, and two long thighs the color of honey. Ah! There she goes, she's starting to size me up with her sexy look; it's because she has readjusted her lips to put her smile back on, a necessary prop in a seducer's paradise. Moumina has for me the face of all the feminine rotundities to grind or knead. Moumina is the human clay on which I dream of planting my particle of life. She's the one who feeds me in the kitchen whenever I feel like eating something. I don't want Maman to know this right away. We feast on the leftovers. Anyway, Moumina's the boss in the kitchen. Let me tell you, I much prefer it this way. Telling you she knows how to be in charge isn't giving away a secret: Moumina grew up in the orphanage managed by the former president's wife. He loved to care for a plentiful, distant brood. Since they were childless, the presidential couple was bled white by their close family, a demanding and expensive one. What more gratifying, then, than a tribe of orphans humming their gratitude, laurel palms in hand, eloquence on their lips, ready to cheer them enthusiastically every single weekend.

3

BASHIR BINLADEN

CALLING YOURSELF Binladen, the most *wanted* man on the planet, it's too-too much, right? Binladen, the biggest rich-killer. His big head with fine-fine beard, most expensive in the world. Worth fifty million dollar. Our new president, old camel pee compared to that. Bush the cowboy president of the Americas want Binladen dead or alive. Also the rich fat-cat Saudis, and his real family, blood of his blood same father same mother, disown Binladen cause they afraid of catching big American revenge. So, Binladen terriblific. But me, I'm mini-Binladen, see, like Madonna dolls, Michael Jackson dolls, the other things there in small-small size. I don't got fine beard and big head of Binladen but watch out, I'm wicked and pitiless. I suicided men, enemy Wadags and other men not enemies. I trashed houses, I drilled girls, I pirated shopkeepers. I pooped in the mosque, but don't shout that from rooftops cause I was very pickled. I done it all. Easy to do things-there when you sleep, you dream, you eat with a Kalashnikov or even an Uzi. Uzi is attack rifle, it's Israeli I'm telling you, believe my word. Israelis too-too strong for war. African heads of state like so-so much Israeli bodyguards cause Israeli bodyguards they protect from military coup like rubber

protect from AIDS you get me? At the front, I was the man who
shot faster than his shadow, Marlboro in my mouth like that,
bazoom bazoom. *Sniper* the Americans say, I saw that in movie
at Youssouf's: Youssouf, he show movies at his house. *Snipers
against Bosnians,* that the name of the movie. They say all the
time Bosnians Muslim, but me I don't believe it cause those
guys have white face an all that.

So, kill, destroy the other side, eat enemies' hearts, OK. By
who? Why? That none of my business. I get my orders, chief
say kill that fat rebel sonofabitch, I kill without fear or fault
cause you gotta obey chief. Way the army is. Our chief got chief
he gotta obey too. Chief of all chiefs on the northern front,
his name Mad Mullah. He drink whiskey in daytime, drink
whiskey at night. When he not drinking whiskey he opening
bottles of beer with the barrel of his AK-47 an yelling orders
quick-quick. I thought about it but I never found out why Mad
Mullah his name. Maybe you know his name-there, his rank,
uniform, his little darlin's perfume an all that. Me I shut my trap
about that cause this business not real clear. Maybe we learn
about that before long.

On the front, lot of us didn't have no uniform. Draftees
cruited quick-quick like me. How old are ya, kid? Eighteen,
I lied for real. Where you from? District 6, Djibouti. You're a
kid from the *magalla,** get over there. Into the courtyard, fall
in! Tomorrow you leave for Yoboki. OK, dismessed. I didn't
even know what to do. I stood planted there front of cruiting
officer. You deaf, or what? Move it! That I know all right. Hour
later, I was in military truck with my new buddies, Ayanleh,
Warya, Aïdid, Haïssama, an all that. Aïdid, that not real name.
Aïdid, he the Somalian general who screwed the American soldiers. Aïdid, champion in battle, Platini[1] of war. Americans,

---

1. Great French soccer player of the 1980s.—*Translators' note*

they making a real movie to show how Aïdid there, he too-too wicked. Aïdid, he got an expensive head, too. Ten million dollars. Our new president flat like old chewed-chewed piece of gum compare to that. No, I say big bravo Aïdid and also he friend with our president not with rebels. Long story short, he no moron like our chief instructor or asshole general now residing in Gabode prison. Yuck.

OK, I gotta confirm this story right away: yes, in the army everyone's not native, plenty cousins from Somalia there. Some come from Mengistu's army, specially with the rebels. There's real foreigners even, I mean *Gaallos**—you know, Whites. Poles, Lebanese or Albanese, Czechoslowhatians an all that. All those guys, they mercenaries like they say in fancy French. But that *top military secret.* I know a real general who helped our president for cheap in great battle of Obock. His name Saxardid, I'm telling the true truth, believe me faithfully, he was second chief of Somalian army with Siyad Barre. Real bloodthirsty one, that guy. Holy shit! Siyad, he was worser than our president who stopped the war. He gobbled little kids not to die old-old. Haile Selassie, he was bigger kid-eater than Siyad Barre with his wife-there, Queen Menem. She liked flesh and fresh blood of children too-too much. So, because of ceasefire, me, I'm demobilized. Not cool, right? Without Kalashnikov you can't pick up rich stuff everywhere no more. That not charity. That civilian life there, it's real shame, you don't scare no one no more. The pretty girls, they boycott you for real. The ugly girls they turn their heads away when you walk in front of their face. The always-unemployed they say out loud hey there's a new unemployed, when before you used to go: bang! boot in the gut here you bastard take that in the belly. Even little mouse laugh at you. City say war no good, no good, like that Congolese singer. But I don't agree. I say war too-too good for sure.

4

ABDO-JULIEN

ALL BLOOD IS MIXED and all identities are nomadic, Maman would have said, talking about me, Papa, herself, or the whole wide world. This business of mixed blood is a very old story, she would add, raising her voice—so old that the first traces of African migration in the Italian peninsula, to give just one example, date from the conquest and fall of Carthage. Much later, there are records of nobles with black slaves: the famous *mori neri* in the paintings of Veronese or Giambattista Tiepolo. All that is typical Maman—a Frenchwoman born in Rennes and attracted by the mixture of races. She came to Djibouti well before I came into the world close to two decades ago. I owe my existence to those student parties that are so popular on campuses. For a few hours, foreign students can forget loneliness, the lack of familiar landmarks, their depression and feeling of dislocation. For a few hours, native students can find cheap thrills, exoticism, the feeling of being transported far away in the sway of the music blaring as loud as possible, and the giddiness caused by the mixture of perfumes and sweat. The Zairian rumba was in full swing then. James Brown, Manu Dibango, and Miriam Makeba heated up their bodies. Later, "Rock

Around the Clock" woke up the ones with a head stewing in hops. The Platters' "Only You" welded the desiring machines together again. Toward dawn, the toughest would stagger back to their rooms with a blood level of alcohol that would make Rasputin turn pale. "It's not because we went there to have a drink or do some dancing that we screwed our balls off," said a friend of my parents who boasts of calling a spade a spade.

My mother, with her hair twisted together like those sentences of Monsieur Proust that no one can unravel, fears neither the sunburns that knock off foreigners with delicate skin nor the narrow little streets covered with dust. As a child I was fed on the milk of love, and reading. The big words of adults went right through my mind (picaresque, epic, tachycardia, scenography, crazy twists and turns of plot . . .), but the stories stayed with me for a very long time. Some day I'll tell you the story of that adventurer from Brittany, born with a fishing rod in his hand, said the novel: he hunted whales in the Bering Straits, sold real Bordeaux wine in the tropics, and took on the boldest pirates with the help of his adorable companion Louison, a royal tigress he had freed from the jaws of a Malaysian crocodile. I still remember every episode. Would you like another one? I'm hesitating between Alexandre Dumas, Eugène Sue, Jules Verne, Scheherazade, or the snow-white beard of Charles Dickens. Are you ready to hunt the rhinoceros in the Serengeti in the company of Ernest Hemingway, become a maharaja in the country of long-haired princes, wind between the seven pillars of wisdom behind Lawrence of Arabia, follow in the footsteps of Peter Pan, or acquire bouquets of wisdom under the guidance of the venerable Tierno Bokar between Dogon cosmogony and Peul poetry? Some other day I'll tell you the life of Monsieur Henri de Monfreid in great detail: Maman loved him at the beginning of her stay in her new country. You're looking at me wide-eyed as if I were a monster, as if I were hiding some shameful infirmity in my frail silhouette. I'm just a little clever for my age, and ahead by a few books. Apparently that happens sometimes: a statistician cites the figure of 1/127, without bothering to prove anything at all. One child out of 127 is supposed to be gifted with superior intelligence—where did he get that stuff? This being said, that little figure might have the advantage of reassuring the most rational minds.

5

BASHIR BINLADEN

WAR'S GOOD FOR LIVING, I mean for making a clean, simple living. How many dead? Why all that? Never again? Forget that debate there, too-too empty. On the front, morale of troops not so good. First of all our chiefs are real morons right out of the Sheraton casino, the greedy Hindi's place. Chiefsthere, OK they pros at restoration, but in battle I give them a flat zero. They bungle it in front of goalposts, right away the enemy screws us in the penalty kick zone an we KO standing up. Worst, every Thursday, they offside. They say yah, we go to the capital, get orders. They give us that to make alibi but they live it up out there at the Sheraton or Tonnelles dance hall inside the thighs of the girls an all. Fridays, they come back tired out like ole boiled chewngum, they stay on the sideline. They don't talk, they fall into big sleep. After that, the Scud, they understood that an fast, cause they had spies in town watching chiefs' little game. Scud, crazy mad for generations. So they attack, bite into the ball like starving hyena. They move down to our side of the field, an us we retreat all the time. So, battle, real simple, like soccer. You retreat, enemy attacks through center and wings. You take a wicked beating. That the story of first half in that civil war-there. Scud scored points. Us, we stuck inside the towns. We play defense in Tadjoura, Obock, Yoboki. When we made little timid attack, bang they sound big alarm. Look, look, they holding population hostage, representatives of the Scud they shout from Yemen and Paris. Open parenthesis. Go fuck self. You got balls, come back to Djibouti. We gonna bomb your Wadag neighborhood of Ambaba. You lousy immigrant bum! Close parenthesis, thanks.

So, us, we defended by kicking the ball out of bounds. We put barbwire an anti-personnel mines all around towns. Daytime, we were the chiefs. Nighttime, they were the *boss*. (That English, I think, right?) It went on like that for the whole first half. Real joke was when president an big politicians in Djibouti they said the Scud not native. They Ethiopian an Eritrean adventurers. On the ground we crack up, we saying in silence: hey president, you ain't ashamed of yaself? Yah yah yah, shut you big mouth! We just say that in silence. Him, the ole president, he had mouth full of bullshit. He came up with big-big words: adventurers, revanchists, illusionists. We listened on Aïdid's radio to Radio France Internationale. (RFI they boast too-too much, they call themselves world radio but who they ask if it true, huh?) Staff sergeant Houmed say in his Tarzan voice: turn that radio off, willya, an fast. The staff sergeant, he was perplex, on one hand he head a battalion of the national army, on the other he was Wadag and supported the rebellion a little, sort of. But he was good chief, honest an all. But wait, things are more complexed than that, Wadags not all rebels. Aïdid for example, his mother Wadag even if he don't understand a thing she say. Haïssima, his father's the Wadag; Haïssima (now that true Wadag name even) he kind of know how to talk patois, that can help in battle. Long story short, let's be serious, half the goverment Wadag. The prime minister of the old president an the new president, the one who been riding horse for a long-long time, Wadag too. He from around Yoboki, I had my first battles there. That where I also did my three months' basic training with real instruction officer, not like the other moron. Where I learned how to march, crawl under barbwire, use weapons, how to prepare ambush, how to pick up secret messages on complicated frequencies (that's how I know secrets, you got that), how to get away before you get wicked red card, etc.

To get back on subject. Oh yah I was saying: Wadags or not Wadags, not the problem. All that's politics, I'm telling you. In a lot of neighborhoods of the capital, in Einguela, Ambouli, Districts 1, 2, 4, Plateau, etc. Wadags, Walals, an Arabs, we all mixed, with plenty Hindis an even some Whites married to our girls, or just weirdos. And then, in the Dikhil district, between Wadags an the others it's *fifty-fifty* (that English, I speak it a little-little. Learned it when I worked in front of the American Embassy, I'll tell you about that later. I know how to talk English an that's that, OK?). So, I was saying: Wadags, tribes an all that, not a problem. Problem is dirty tricks, corruption an politics. You know, Restoration! When I was in the belly of my departed mama, they say: yah yah Wadags too-too mean. Ali Aref, the chief of goverment cabinet right under white chief (High Commissioner of the Republic, that's how they called him. Me, I thought Republic was only the name of boulevard in Djibouti), he was Wadag and used to kill all the Walals who worked for independence. All the young guys supposed to be activists, they pigged out on a bullet in the belly nice an quick. Next morning they find the bodies naked in the mangrove swamp, near the supermarket. The old politicians under thumb of the colonialists they went yum-yum in the Chamber of Deputies. So Ali Aref and his clique they civil goverment and the Walal chiefs (hey, not all!) they the rebels. Me I say, don't throw oil on the fire. Gotta stop that talk-there. All that, just ole folks stuff. Us, we don't care. Anyways, we weren't alive yet, we were in Mama's belly wriggling around all the time waiting our turn to come outside mama. You remember what was going on when you were inside your mama? So there!

6

ABDO-JULIEN

I'M CURIOUS about everything. As soon as the door opens
a crack, I slip like a little mouse into Papa's library, where the
caramel smell of his Amsterdamer is floating in the air, and
search through the jumble of papers and newspaper cuttings.
Old copies of the *Réveil*, recent issues of *La Nation*, the gov-
ernmental weekly, communiqués of the Scud that reach him
through secret channels, *l'Ensemble* of the Fearless Opponent
and the brand new regional bimonthly *Nouvelles du Pount* that
friends brought from Paris are all piled up on the floor. It's a
shambles. Oh, and there's an old adage—I don't remember
who wrote it: tell me what's in your library and I'll tell you
who you are. But enough of that. I unfold a newspaper and I go
through it for hours on end. It puts a stop to teenage games and
laughter with my neighborhood buddies, the family of Papa's
colleague Guelleh Hersi included. I really don't care. I hardly
register fifteen on the speedometer and I'm not done telling
you my crazy stories. Once I've finished reading the papers I
stay there dreaming for a while. These are the times when my
mind rises and frees itself from all its bonds. It whirls around
so deliriously I grow faint. It's an aircraft carrier where only

fertile mirages take off, a cloud-bird huge as a whole world. Through the twisting, mysterious paths of my imagination, I often succeed in linking some of the names repeated in the newspapers to street names I manage to decode on the few commemorative plaques that are still legible, or to the names I catch in the course of an argument between adults. No way I'll interpret an anecdote or the fragment of a story I intercept here and there as a single piece of music, a score established once and for all. I now know (but who can ever be sure with me—you're so singular and evanescent, Papa would say) that Aboubaker Aref and Houmed Dini are among the first important people who went to sign agreements with the Emperor Napoleon over a hundred and fifty years ago. I also know that Grandpa used to play just one record—but what a record! Oum Kalsoum giving a masterly interpretation of *Anta Oumri:* sixty minutes of pure bliss. I noted that the Bank of Suez on Place Menelik, where my parents go so often—my father, once again, would say that some adults draw the water of their own well-being from the success of their clan—has something to do with a story that fascinated me for weeks on end: the odyssey of the Frenchman Ferdinand de Lesseps opening the canal of the same name through his pugnacity, trickery, and flexible spine. But did I know that the fiery lawyer who just yesterday publicly challenged the authorities in Djibouti is also a descendant of the pasha that Napoleon invited over for tea? The name Napoleon sounds like an animated cartoon character lost in a fabulous land like Tarzan's savannah, Aladdin's magic lamp, or the enchantments of *The Jungle Book.* My two special heroes are Peter Pan and Don Quixote; Grandpa admired Saad Zaghloul, the Egyptian who headed the revolt against the English in 1919, I think, led his country to liberation and truly deserved his great equestrian statue in the middle of Alexandria.

I navigate easily between different languages, historical references, cultures, rumors from yesterday still warm today, and the oldest memories. Totally natural, I'm the product of love without borders; I'm a hyphen between two worlds. But wait, I'm not just a contemplative mind; I'm interested in others, in my family first of course, but also in everybody. Thus my repeated insistent winks to Moumina—ah, I'd love to say "*Ya habibi*"* to her some day, like in the sweet songs of Oum Kalsoum. And ride her mane. She would be Eve (or Hawa) and I would be Adam (or Aden). Together we would Adamandeve around a brand new world where life would be generous to everyone, where every moment would be a ceremony. Not to mention the discreet helping hand I give to my neighbors and buddies Kahen and Koschin with their homework. And when there are too many clouds in the blueing sky, the first words of a song Maman often listens to come back to me right away. It begins with Serge Gainsbourg's *Dieu est un fumeur de havanes* ("God smokes a Havana cigar") and then gets lost in the mist, of course. I can't help thinking how much she probably misses the wind-rain of her Brittany but I keep quiet. Maman's irrepressible laughter when she pretends to be Janis Joplin comes back to me right away.

7

BASHIR BINLADEN

THE FIRST HALF lasted long-long time in that war. Everybody stayed in position; the attacks were rare. The battle was a tie, without real fair referee. Cause referee still France in that business-there. Paul Djidou, the Paris guy, never stop coming an going between Paris an Djibouti, so much the Boeing 747 all tired out. Paul Djidou he mediation: result zero. But goverment accuse: yes you wanna help the rebels, France too much friend of The Eternal Opponent (Eternal Opponent, he new chief of Scud, sworn enemy of the president, former prime minister, former deputy, former nurse—Eternal Opponent always former). On their side the rebels accuse too: yes, France providing support for the maneuvers (that military language, very correct) of the goverment. Paul Djidou yelled: yes me too I'm sick of this former territory of Wadags and Walals, and hey I'm going back to Nice (Nice, it beautiful part of France). Long-long time later we learn on RFI that Monsieur Paul Djidou, he left to do peace mediation between Hutus and Tutsis, over there in Rwanda, I think. Results: first half of the first war, it lasted. Old as a child of three, an that no joke. Both teams, they thought we gonna find new fair referee. Eternal Opponent went to ask

Saleh (no, not the marathonian from Djibouti, that Ahmed Saleh, he so-so good with feet; the other Saleh, he president of Yemen) if he think he can be good fair referee. Saleh said: that political interference. Me too, I got big problems: with Eritrea, with fierce bearded guys (poor Saleh don't know my name been Binladen for six months, that confidential top military secret). Real country of Binladen, it's not Gaudy Arabia, sorry, Saudi Arabia, it's Yemenite mountains. Binladen before he got rich an smart he was living out in the sticks in Yemen. So Saleh of Yemen he end up saying go see UN, OAU, Arab League, you'll find good fair referee. So war will stop by itself. Dialogue between goverment and Eternal Opponent is deaf dialogue, always. Us draftees, we were happy. We had the weapons, the right to do whatever we want. An then, there still wasn't fierce battle. It was status quo (that military language too). Tie. And lots of dead too, specially rebels or civilians who sort of help rebels. But wait, let's be serious, there dead on our side too, specially young draftees with no esperience, not like me or Aïdid, Warya, Ayanleh, Haïssama. Lot of young draftees (why'm I saying young draftees, they all young, right?) pig out on bullets in the belly. That's war, but can't cry too much like mamas. Man with real hard thing between his legs never cry like little woman and that's that. Dismessed.

8

ABDO-JULIEN

I THINK THE DEAD are not dead but go on with their little lives, only on another planet. When the evening wind comes in with its troubling scythe, someone you love leaves you. Death should not be proud; people do not die, they just become invisible. God, it's so cold alone here in the grave, they whisper. Like that grandmother from ancient times with the face of a great sachem, affectionate and despotic, who died in her eighty-fifth year, well, she's walking along over a dried-out wadi on the Moon with her long, majestic stride, hampered by a double pain in the hip. She could read the future in the flight of birds and would raise her head to search the stars and the Moon at every occasion. Ah, she could see herself on that lunar land inhabited by old people, stunted acacias, a natural world in suspension or in miniature, bony camels, cats with stringy coats, cacti with a fragile constitution. Life is not abundant there, it's a break in the clouds, but peace reigns permanently and men have lost their vanity and their destructive energy. Every man bears witness for humanity. Besides, don't they whisper behind my back that I, Abdo-Julien, am the reincarnation of my grandfather, who was assassinated by a thug in the Foreign

Legion? Grandfather often comes to visit me. Over there, in the country where he is, they don't call children "children" but "the ones with small feet"; men are companions of the Sun, the other point of reference, along with the Moon—Earth has been utterly forgotten. Round, white flat stones are found there in great numbers, like on a beach of the alabaster coast between Dieppe and Étretat, where I spent a few days during my last summer vacation in Maman's part of the country. Bristling with volcanic knolls, the earth of the Moon seems plunged in a long eternal sleep just slightly smoothed by the sand winds that surge up out of nowhere. The companions of the Sun have slept peacefully, with a clear conscience, ever since they let the people on Earth be born, die, and be born again wherever they are, do their thing and walk round and round inside the circle of their well-fed sedentariness. They remain at the mercy of a big, violent current that will swallow them up forever. Speaking of the ones on the Moon like Grandpa Awaleh, they fit into their new existence with the ease of an alley cat. They're like flying leaves fluttering in the arms of the wind; their own horizon loses its weight and sways along on its wings without a trace or a final point. They are humble; they are able to love slowness and appreciate the wisdom of former times. They have left our wretched enclosures forever. They're not struggling along any more under the constant threat of earthquake in the country of dead stones.

I learned all that from Grandpa, who would tell it to me during his unexpected visits. Experience is a lantern on your back, he would teach me when I asked him a tough question; it only lights up the path behind you. It's weird, these days his face is round and soft, with no hard cheekbones or tense muscles. A face like the Moon.

9

BASHIR BINLADEN

SO I GOT TOO-TOO MAD. Let's get real here. You think
people walk with their ass on the ground? We hear the rebels
almost in Djibouti and us, we stuck here, in mountain. They
gonna waste everybody over there. When they gonna give the
order to attack Scud positions? They say president he don't give
a damn about anything, homeland, fatherland, population. He
too-too old. So he left for vacation in Parisian hospital after
rest in private villa-chateau cause now it's *haga** (that Djibouti
summer, sun it hot lead melting on your skull, even the asphalt
on the road yell mama mama I'm too-too melted). *Haga,* too
fierce. All the *leaders* (that use to be English before, now not
so sure) they left to rest up in Paris, Switzerland, Washimton
(for the big somebodies), Addis, Cairo, Yemen (for the small
fry—that cook language, Ayanleh who was student cook for the
Whites before mobilization told me that). And us, we famished
an languished on bald mountain there. We bite our nails cause
of nothing to do. Gotta attack Scud making too many corner
kicks, an beat it up a little, I say. Gotta hit Scud in Achilles' heel.
But that little chief of us, he don't agree. You need green light
from chiefa staff even, he answer. Man! We ain't out of this yet.

Little chief of us with walkie-talkie an old VHF radio (cause big chief need Motorola cell, of course) he don't agree at all. You think we having fun here? We maintaining the blockade so the rebels are cut off from urban centers. Bullshit. For long time now, Scud been getting supplies from the sea with fast little patrol boats getting ammunition and 9mm in Yemen, that not even confidential top military secret. Even some wounded rebels, they get treated in Peltier Hospital in Djibouti cause they got cousins in goverment too. Me I say all that business shady-shady. He who has ears, let him hear, cept maybe the phony deaf. The country's future's dot-dot-dot suspension points so you gotta think real hard. When war's over, I look for nice chic job. Yes, I know profession like that, it real job front of American Embassy or Mitterrand Consulate, yes. But hey, that my secret.

10

ABDO-JULIEN

THERE! We're all together again now, by the grace of the Most Lofty. Let's chat for a few moments. I'll go back to what I was telling you yesterday, my boy. So, where was I? Oh yes, did you know that the nomads are late converts, that Islam is an urban religion, born among merchants from Mecca? It is true that Mohammed, may his soul rest in peace, succeeded in conquering the nomads, regimenting them in his troops and sending them forth to conquer the world. And do you know that our beloved religion never really took to the sea, which is why Muslim societies have lagged behind in the development of capitalism? Islam has always viewed sailors as people on the fringe of society, outcasts, or rebels. Now, you little rascal, you're going to ask me how I can explain the power of Oman, if only in our region, and the advent of Swahili civilization from the Red Sea to the Mozambique Channel. It's due to prehistoric maritime cultures. The Omanese and a few Turkified populations on the banks of the Black Sea were able to preserve this knowledge of the sea, and so those remarkable sailors and fishermen gave birth to a veritable maritime power in the Indian Ocean. You didn't know that either, did you? Beware of appearances: an imposture may even lie between the pages of a history book made in Paris. Now listen to me. No, it's not hard to reach out to people. On the contrary, people are dying to find an attentive ear willing to listen to them and a mind inclined to stir up the mulch of their understanding. From time immemorial, Grandfather gave every conversation a certain depth, a duly calculated slowness that had absolutely nothing to do with laziness. There was in his gestures, and especially in his voice, an economy that captivated and galvanized me by its gentleness, its rhythm, and by the way he would stretch out a vowel like *o* or *u*, depending on his argumentation. And every one of his actions was marked by the same relaxed intensity. He did not hesitate to ask my grandmother Timiro for his thermos of tea three times in a row without raising or lowering his voice. And in the same courteous, firm tone, he could also insist that Grandmother make the tea over again if he didn't like the way it was brewed. All this not for the pleasure of indisposing others and showing his authority like the old quibblers of his age, nor to bother anyone, just to make sure that his interlocutors fully understood all his rights, even in the state of physical helplessness he was in before he passed from life to death. For him, life was a constant flow of exchanges in words or deeds, and because of this, he took all the time he needed to pose his voice, give his opinions, and move his old bones. Without haste, he tasted the sap of every minute: life is a banquet to be savored together, no need to lap it up in two strokes of a spoon. Not everyone shared his point of view. Timiro, gripped by the feeling of his precariousness, often let a few tears escape: they flowed down the ridge of her nose and flooded the hills of her cheekbones.

Real creators are stateless wanderers, like the nomads of the desert, and have only one function—at least in this world below. They are our guides (Grandfather is convinced of this) who show us the trails to follow as we travel through life. They also tell us, with an abundance of details, the story of their emotional carousel. With their memory zinzoling here and there, their imagination working in geometric shapes—rectangles, triangles, trapezoids—they spare us muddy streams, the foaming slime of remorse, putrid waters like the waters of Lake Abbé, even the raging sea. The sea with its gums of an ogre so frightening to mankind. With these guides, you feel like pouncing on that Reaper, taking a dive into that hell which attracts men so much. Chroniclers of the ephemeral, they shell their sayings like oysters; they have such airborne words that they set off levitation above senses and sentiments. Silence and pandemonium bumping into each other, negating each other. The sudden blooming of new knowledge. They offer us pearls of rain from countries where it never rains, as Jacques Brel says in his song, major chords that connect man to humanity. As long as they can speak to us, their voices are made flesh, connecting us to others. They are herders of cows or dromedaries, crossers of limits, peddlers of mirages dragging behind them the latest news of the evening. They own nothing solid, or so little. Bitter almonds and sounds of bones, for many. For others, just a sheepskin for prayer and gymnastics for the believer. And when night has burned out the oil of its last lamps, one must make haste: it is the autumn of life. Poets approaching death commonly become prophets.

11

BASHIR BINLADEN

THE FIRST HALF not over and already part of Scud and the president began negotiations. It's simple: three Scud chiefs left for the capital. They say contact was still prime minister, the one who gets off his horse just to pee. Bégé (that's his name for short like RPP—that the name of the one an only party—an like RFI, PSG,[1] etc.), he from same region as three chiefs, their name still top military secret. But OK, I can give you a hint, one's called Kif-Kif something, all the same. That don't mean a thing to you, don't matter too-too much. The man not well-known like me Binladen that's all. The three chiefs, they gonna hug the old president. And him, he gonna give armchair, residence, vehicle, official position an all that. Business-there, it Scud number 1, you got it. TV, radio, Peace Day everywhere. Dances (funny to have war dances to celebrate peace, no?), khat, and speeches. Even Madame President she was dancing in front of crowd full of bodyguards. Nobody thought about us, out there on the mountain facing enemy. Luckily everybody

---

1. PSG: Paris Saint-Germain, a famous professional soccer team.—*Translators' note*

has their Kalashnikov. But wait, there's old Kalash an modern Kalash, see. Old Kalash is AK-47, modern is AK-58, tricky cause it sprays quick-quick. If it falls down, it fires by itself. AK-47 it can fall, it can trample an all but it stay calm cause of safety lock. AK-58 safety lock so-so small, tiny, way it is, it's danger of death. There's also machine-gun, rocket launchers, mortars, ground-to-ground (all that too-too heavy to carry). Better not walk behind buddy with rocket launcher, danger of death too. OK, rebels always attack when they very-very hungry. They come out of the brush, hide next to tar road, wait for vehicles. Unity Road (that the main Djibouti-Tadjoura road also called Fahd bin Abdulaziz Road, that the name of Saudi prince who gifted the road) that max danger cause rebels they not only looking for food, they want khat too, that way they be brave to make ambush again. Us we wait for official order to clean up all that. Well, we gonna wait long-long time cause Scud 1 an President lovey-dovey now. They smooch like women or Soviet chiefs I saw on Samireh the shopkeeper's TV. Ah, politics too-too ugly. Shameful, for real. What the three Scud 1 chiefs like Kif-Kif (Kif-Kif, Habachi, that Ethiopian name or what?) gonna tell their bambinos (that correct Italian, right?) They gonna say hey we happy, we signed negotiations in Abaro, we made peace. The kids, they gonna say whew with their hands on their mouths. Big, big shame. Aïdid, he say politics too-too dumb even. I agree, politicians useless losers who don't know how to do anything, don't know how to be mechanic, cook, teacher, doctor. Don't even know how to stand guard. Hey, I hear a lot of metal noises. Time to eat. Hunger hasn't fled my body even if sleep left my eyes since I tasted the pink pills Aïdid has in his pocket. I wanna gobble something cause my belly's going grrr grrr.

12

ALICE

THIS WAS AT THE TIME when there were still straw huts (*ar-iches*, they're usually called) on the main street, Boulevard de Gaulle today—our beloved France hadn't yet taken the hammering it got in 1940—the last huts of this kind disappeared at the turn of the seventies, just before we arrived here. The name Boulaos remains, at the spot of the first fishing village. Dromedaries laden with bundles of sticks and saddled donkeys carrying water would often parade through the main streets of what was still called the native village—the *magalla*—which would steadily expand through the years. In Ambouli, there was also a zoo facing the palm grove. A wind turbine towered majestically over it; a crowd of children rushed there every afternoon like beggars charging at a cigarette butt that someone just threw away.

All that was yesterday, at the time when Alfred Ilg and Léon Chefneux had just launched the train, and the cathedral was still the church Sainte-Jeanne-d'Arc; it was roughed up by the earthquakes of 1929, 1930, and 1942. A whole yesterday still fresh in my mind, not your time, my little cactus, but rather the time of your father when he was still a teenager. You'd think

47

it's already been relegated to time immemorial, like the women who sorted coffee beans on Place Ménélik; today they'd be as old as your grandmother. Or the time of the native militia (your grandfather was one of its first recruits). With the help of the Senegalese infantrymen—in reality not only Senegalese but from all over the AOF[1]—they maintained order in the model city, as model as a sub-prefecture of Ardèche or Ariège in France, or at least that was the claim of the weekly paper of the colony, whose banknotes came from the Banque de l'Indochine. During that whole period, they particularly had to keep their eyes on the Place des Chameaux (the future Place Rimbaud, now Place Mahmoud-Harbi, a stone's throw from the great Hammoudi mosque, which symbolized Djibouti and the Côte Française des Walals at the famous Paris Colonial Exposition of 1931). It served as the terminal for caravans but also as the main market for wood, milk, butter, and the spicy rumors from the backcountry, so dreaded by the governor. As soon as he got up in the morning, the governor would inquire into what was being said on the Place des Chameaux, who had arrived that day, what could have been said about him, what would Paris think of his silence, it's been three days since he didn't send them a letter through the usual channels. A colonial intelligence agent, relying on his three informers from the native tribes, would reassure him immediately. Nothing to worry about as far as our interests are concerned, the same old stories of bloodshed, poisoned wells, kidnapped fiancées, raids on zebus, and vendettas between rival clans. Trouble could come from the greed of the Abyssinians, but we've known that for ages. So, a promising day for the governor despite the blazing sun, so hot it could addle the brains of the little blond heads of the schoolchildren in the École de la Nativité. And the aroma

1. Afrique Occidentale Française, French West Africa.—*Author's note*

of coffee would attract the governor. A table was set under the oleanders for this ritual. He would go inspect the brand-new premises of the Messageries Postales built by Duparchy and Vigoureux, the same firm that had put the final touch on all the viaducts between Djibouti and Addis Ababa as early as 1897, making generous use of metallic constructions of the Eiffel type. In short, a real day's work.

There was in our house a dog-eared sepia photograph sitting on a piece of furniture in the living room. You could see Mahmoud Harbi with a baby face, although he had already turned thirty, in a suit, with a bow tie. A baby face because it's only after they've reached forty-four that men here are fully entitled to be called an adult, your grandfather would have said in his gentle voice. Whoever entered the living room could not fail to take off his hat before that heroic figure. Could the dead really be the only creatures to inspire respect and dignity in this world here below? Behind the photo, on the wall, a map of Greater Somalia would attract the visitor's attention. A sand-yellow territory on a sky-blue background, and all around it the four colonialists (France, Great Britain, Italy, and Ethiopia) who cut up the land of the sons of Samaale. That very allegorical map was less appreciated than the photo of the great fighter.

13

BASHIR BINLADEN

THE OLD-OLD SOLDIERS, ones thirty an over, they loved strong liquor too-too much: gin, vodka, Johnny Walker, White Spirit. It's top chief brings back that stuff. Fat rich Arabs and Hindis, they give all that free for the patriotic effort. No lies that. Label say so. Établissement Fratacci, El Gamil Supermarket, Borreh & Associates, Idriss Driving School, V. D. Singh & K. S. Vijay, Coubèche and Sons, etc., see what I mean? Rebels they love *doomo* too much (that, Wadag palm wine). Us young draftees, we like liquor not too-too strong. Heineken, Kronenbourg, Tuborg, plus pink pills plus hashish. w o w w! After that, sleep flee from your eyes. Belly stop fussing, that's all. You can't fish up pity for nobody, not even for a small-small little child. You pick up rebels' girls to make slave honeys in military camp. All the girls, they're for us, they gotta show their ass, that simple. Some girls they even come on purpose, they leave the mountain, they too-too hungry. They say: I wanna stay with soldiers, there's army food. They love soldiers for that, or else it's hunger too much. Rebels, when they gain ground on us, they catch their sisters. They knock em off quick-quick. Yah, you were with soldiers. You traitors, you cooked for soldiers, you screwed all the time. Bitches, I'm gonna fuck up your life: here, take that in the ass and bang! And you after that, you go crazy. You don't give a shit; you throw the old mamas old uncles and all in holes in the mountain singing Tupac Shakur. You burn camp; you poison water. You spray the animals bang-abangbang. It's funny, camel stuffed with bullets falls, gets up on long-long legs, falls, gets up, falls, up again. You come in bang bang bang salaam-an-bye-bye. Who gives a shit? Cows, they too stupid, they got big white eyes, moo moo moo, they wait for the bullets, they looking for death. Sheep, they run all over. Goats, they run-run fast. I saw soldiers rape donkey going ee ... ee ... ee. You have a ball.

When work there done, you burn your hash, you breathe in hard-hard till your eyes pop out of your face. After that, you calm, you cool with your Walkman. You can't stand tiny-tiny noise. So you sleep. Not for long. Two hours max; after, it's sentry duty. The others they sleep two hours and then, sentry duty. That way, you get used to it. You just take little nap cept when you smoked too much, grazed too much khat. But OK, that your own business. When chief he ask, Bashir you been smoking again? No Sir Sergeant, I give answer all ready. Always deny that stuff-there. Chief, he can't do nothing, he needs draftees to go on details too much. To get the prisoners together, bury wounded quick, burn rebel corpses covered with white clay (must be their grigri, that), it's the rule here. And soldier, he follow rules an that's that.

The night after, you have nightmare plus nightmare all night. Once, I had mean nightmare. We were trapped in ambush near Kallafi. Aïdid, Ayanleh, Haïssama, they dead. Me, I hid behind acacia. The rebels, they look all over. They don't find me. Then, at the last minute, a smart little rebel he found hiding place. Now four rebels coming in, their finger on trigger. They come up slow-slow like Clint Easthoud in movie (shit, this is serious, man, I can't remember what movie). They keep coming at me. OK I got my Kalash; I keep cool. They come closer. They look lef-right; they come closer. Shit, my Kalash, it stuck, don't wanna work. The four rebels, they see my Kalash it screwed. Me too.

14

ABDO-JULIEN

GRANDFATHER USED TO SAY: the desert you see there, well,
it's alive, like you and me. Proof is, the dunes are white in their
childhood and grow yellow over the centuries. To see it, all you
have to do is put on the right kind of glasses or stand at the right
distance. Nothing ever dies, and the desert you see there can
regain its former face, the face of the savannah, go back to the
sea of water and grass, the way it was a few million years ago.
Clock time and hourglass time are nothing, absolutely nothing,
compared to the age of the globe. In the same way, man's path
is not linear like the horizon: it has roots, branches, and sap. It's
all renewal, rhizomes, and ramifications. Man is a tree, my boy.
I hardly listen to him; he's been talking by himself for hours.
A hundred billion neurons, what a capital! But very few people
draw generously from this capital Providence has bestowed on
us—not to mention the evils of khat, alcohol, tobacco, and the
intoxication of arms. Men are brainless hunks of meat; I almost
choke when I say that to you. A star falls from my eyes, they're
suddenly misty, a tear is putting a pearl on my wrinkled cheek.
It is time for me to go away and leave you to your daydreams,

my boy. I'll come back tomorrow and we'll pick up the discussion exactly where we left off.

My grandfather used to tell me a story he'd told Papa and the many cousins and grand-nephews. The family and the tribe are all mixed together. With us, the tribe is a compact crowd, a whole people. But before telling his story, all of a sudden he would be off, far away, as if he were on the Balbala bus. Then he would come back to the beginning and tell us his story. We would savor it like fresh milk from the udders of a cow. Grandfather was unpredictable. Grandpa, you're like those women who want to be loved right away, someone would say without raising his hand, like at the Muallim school.[1]

"Do you know that the crazy planispheres of the fifteenth century put the earthly paradise—a paradise surrounded by flames, of course—on the exact spot where Abyssinia is located, that is, here in our country?"

And he would turn around and tell his story.

"I'm going to tell you the story right away. It's an old Arab tale. Zakaria Tamer of Syria cooked it up like a chef. One day in the Alep bazaar, a man bought two big eggs from a grocer. He was very hungry. He put an egg in each pocket, politely refusing the bag that the grocer held out for him. Once he got home, he ran to the kitchen and took out a plate and a frying pan. He broke the first egg against the second one. Out came a little chick all covered with down. Mad with rage, he was cursing the sly grocer who had deprived him of his omelet when suddenly his heart sank down to his feet, for the chick began to grow and soon took on the shape of a man with two wings, a pleasant face, and loose, white clothing. He took fright, invoked the name of The Unique, and dropped the second egg. Out came a chick all

---

1. Koranic school.—*Translators' note*

covered with down, who quickly grew and took the shape of a man who looked exactly like the first. What could he do, what could he say? He girded up his loins:

"'Good God, who are you?'

"'I am Munkir,' said the first. 'And he is Nakir.'

"Then he added, with authority:

"'You must have heard of us. At your age, you certainly should have. We are the two angels who visit a dead person during the first night he spends in the grave in order to draw up the balance sheet of everything he has done on earth.'

"'So why have you come? Can't you see I am not dead? Or do you want to tangle with me? I am a boxer, and in all of Alep and beyond, and even in Palmyra people know the force of my fists.'

"'Do not be angry, brave boxer,' said Munkir in a sincerely sorry voice. 'There must be some mistake. Accept our apology.'

"And Nakir apologized sincerely to him, too. Then they both walked towards the door.

"'Where are you going?' cried the man, blocking their way.

"'Much work still awaits us,' answered Munkir.

"'What about my eggs? Who's going to reimburse me for them?'

"'Well, you see . . .' stammered Nakir.

"'It is quite simple. Pay me,' suggested the hungry man.

"Munkir held up his arms:

"'Search our pockets; we possess nothing. Nothing earthly, at least.'

"The man refused to let them go. He did not want to remain without food because of a mistake other people had committed, even if they were well-intentioned.

"'Be reasonable, we have no money,' begged Nakir.

"'We could help you out a bit on Judgment Day,' added Munkir.

"'By overlooking some of your bad deeds,' said Nakir.

"The man thought for half a minute and then reluctantly accepted. He pointed a firm forefinger at the angels:

"'You give me your word as men?'

"The angels fluttered their wings in sign of protest.

"The man hastened to correct himself:

"'I meant, your word as angels!'

"And the angels nodded and slipped away."

15

BASHIR BINLADEN

CIVILIANS, they not happy with us cause of the patriotic contribution. The goverment, it put 27 percent of pay direct into its
pocket to support the war. So goverment employees, they look
at us mean. Me, I don't agree. It's not cause of draftees you got
war they call civil. It's war that called up draftees. So let's get
serious and not put the cart before the cow, right? And then, all
the money they get don't go to draftees; first it go into the big
guys' pockets. Proof is, they all build big villa-chateaus like the
president. Even goverment employee who's insignificant (that,
estremely good word even), he wants a little villa-chateau same
as big chief of the Republic. Me I don't give a shit about tears of
lazybone employees, if they not happy they can go knock their
head against the wall. Or else revolt, but that, I don't think so,
cause of khat. Khat make you talk-talk, dream-dream, and then
zero in the brainbox. Khat, it put body energy to sleep. Even
men's thing there, it floppy like old chewed-chewed gum. So
revolt not around the corner I'm telling you.

Aïdid, he don't agree with me. He say, revolution, it can come
tomorrow. In Somalia, they kicked out Siyad Barre and they
graze khat too but hey, less than Djibouti. Djibouti, great graz-

ing champs after Yemenites. Yemenites, they close their eyes.
They graze, graze, an graze. Sleep flee the eyes of Yemenites.
Sleep forgot there are Yemenites on our nice little planet. After Yemenites, me I say second Djibouti, third Somalia, fourth
Ethiopians. But Habashis don't graze, see, they drink *buna** in
the daytime and *taji** at night. Aïdid no dope. He got a point.
We can revolt like Somalians too, but wait, you gotta know how
to stop a war. In Mogadishu, the asshole generals like Aïdid
(not my buddy, the real chief who screwed the Americans and
filmed American corpse pulled by kids and dragged all over
town with women whooping—shame, for braggy Americans
an Clinton!) and consorts, they been fighting for years. Not
a good idea to do that too-too much here at home. Nice little
revolt to correct things, OK. Anyways, it's all over for the asshole general of police, the one sleeping presently in the sinister
Gabode prison. Next time it'll work, inshallah. And me, I'll
have something to do with that business-there. But that still
confidential top military secret.

16

AWALEH

LET'S NOT FORGET that we never accepted the domination of the colonizers. Even when faced with a fait accompli and the law of the strongest, we resisted silently, secretly.

Luckily, we had enough space to fall back on, unlike countries with greater population density like Burundi or Rwanda, where the Catholic church recorded its highest evangelization scores in the world. We could retreat into the brush, unseen and unheard. And above all, no official papers. Thus, what seemed to be the most generous acts of the administration, like the vaccination campaigns, were ignored if not massively rejected. Villages, schools, or cities—we rejected them. We preferred our rustic life.

But as time went on, those of us who had settled in little towns along the Djibouti–Addis Ababa railroad line got caught up in the game and first sent a little boy, some little orphan, to their school just out of curiosity. Then the youngest boy of the family, then the middle son, and finally the eldest, the keeper of the flock. But what could the children be doing all day? ventured the most skeptical. Faithful as the evening stars, they went to the same place every day, remaining seated, filling out little spiral notebooks with the district chief's stamp on them, and came back a few years later with a salary, without breaking their backs. Their fathers immediately opened up a store. From then on, they would rent out the donkey they used to lend. Little by little, they cut themselves off from their clan, spoke about their ancestors for no good reason, and were reluctant to give out alms. They shut themselves off from the others and saw only people like themselves, or passing foreigners like the nurse or the stationmaster, French from France or Greeks. And finally the truck driver replaced the camel driver, already threatened by the train.

17

ABDO-JULIEN

IF WE ARE TO BELIEVE Grandfather, the Moon is even rounder in the neighbor's sky, the grass always cooler in the field next door. Be that as it may, you mustn't run the risk of getting your throat cut by the sabers of the madmen who belch out their sayings and skim the city. They have forgotten the injunction the Angel gave the Prophet in a cave on Mount Hira. It said: "*Iqrah!* Recite!" From this verb comes the word Koran, recitation. At that time, reading, or recitation, was something very different from the present droning of the Word weakened by narrow minds, often bearded. *Iqrah,* recite and think by yourself, expand your knowledge; seek, in the bottom of your heart, the path that leads to The Unique. According to Muslim tradition, the revelation of the Koran by the archangel Djibril was a long ordeal—they seem to have forgotten that these days—constant, but painful and fragmented, scaled up over more than twenty-three stations with new additions, adjustments, and successive corrections. That long quest, the goal of a whole life, bears its beginnings and endings within it. "Here, Adam remembers the dust of his clay," says the poet Mahmoud Darwish. Who, better than the poet, can rise to the divine?

Certainly not the shouters who claim that monopoly for themselves. "As for poets, they are followed only by those who have lost their way. Seest thou not that they stray distracted in every valley? And that they say what they do not do?" (the Koran).

18

BASHIR BINLADEN

IF I TAKE PINK PILLS, my head too-too light. And if I see something, I want that thing, I take it right away even if it my mother's thing or president's. Us draftees, we fierce like that. And my poor head it flies all by itself like helicopter. In helicopter you're not so scared, you a little far up in the sky. You can piss on enemy's head. So, you're not scared unless the other guy, he has rocket launchers, ground-to-ground an all that. That the way French army turned over our heads. Tuck-tuck-tuck-tuck Gazelle helicopters went all the time to spy on our positions an then, deal intelligence with enemy. You could even see Mirage F1's flying by right near us, like this: zzzzzzoooooooffff. We didn't say much cause us, we don't have AMX tanks an fast furtive patrol boats (that real correct, I know) to mix it up with French military. French military, we call em FFDJ (French Forces stationed in Djibouti) in professional lingo. So, that the way Scud 2 gained ground after they sign peace with their old buddies in Scud 1. We weren't too mad cause battle our job. But the president, he real-real mad. Scud 2 stronger than Scud 1. Scud 2, they strong like Rivaldo, the midfielder who feeds guys a lot of shots at goal in Spanish championship. Scud brave even, cause rebels now they drive Toyota pickups loaded with antimissile batteries and lot of heavy weapons. We call those bizarre tanks-there *technicals* (that English, I think). It's Somalians invented that technique, Somalians strong for war like Eritreans, like Rwandese of Kagame (Africans, poor but strong for war, right?). So, Scud 2 they got new weapons, easy to show courage with new terriblific weapons.

President with very-very mad face, he went to France, he went to Soodi Arabia, he went to Switzerland, he went to China, all that to ask for money for top modern weapon an equipment. President, he too-too nervous, gonna die of heart attack cept if God change his heart. On the ground you can feel his big anger cause chiefs don't stop yelling on our back. After that he brought much more draftees into army, even children too young, they children an soldier both, see. These kids they so-so scared cause their chiefs they make em suffer very-very much to obliterate easy life of before. When they go into battle first time, they say: you, kid, go kill off wounded rebel-there, and they give him a pistol to go tockatockatocka. After, they give good hard wash to kid's face with blood of rebel wounded or dead. When little soldier he learns courage and gets fierce, then he can fire bazooka easily at mama papa uncle cousin muezzin an all, believe me faithfully. Little soldier, he too-too dangerous all the time cause he mix up game and battle. He mix life an death with big smile on his face. OK, even with small-small soldiers there, Scud 2 still gaining ground. The goverment they say if Scud 2 winning many battles it's cause French spies gave away plan with lot of information. French spies told em positions, weapons, numbers an all. A goverment like that, debacle they say in military language. Too terrible, even.

19

ABDO-JULIEN

ONE, TWO, THREE, WOWWWWW! We're the Mau-Mau, a group of young musicians in love with whirling, turbulent music from the depths of the desert. Blues, *guux,** *gabay,** and *geeraar.** Wowwwwwwwww! We left the city to collect all the sonorities, the overflowing saps, sounds, singularities, songs, noises, tempests, and myths of the country. We went still farther. Alternative rock, reggae, *rai,* rap, ragamuffin, ska, and *sega* music hold no secrets for our muddy, moody, and even booted feet. We're the generation who sucked Jamaican music with the milk of our bottle; our birth coincides with the death of the long-haired prince who made the island of the Rastas world-famous. We seek the hypnosis of rhythm, language, song. The art of jubilation. You either are a revolutionary or you'll never be one, said old Victor Hugo. Our greatest reward is when we succeed in making old bodies of forty reel, like our parents, by playing them a piece of salsa, yesterday's *pachanga,* or a wild rumba, reminding them of the time when they were students abroad. Their tired eyes stare at the corner of a street, a sea horizon, and the unknown that lies at the end of it, a slice of life between Saint-Germain and Montparnasse. Thus we mix generations together—no small deal in this country of ours. We delve far, far down into the mysteries of the past; we bring up yesterday's ashes, delaying tactics and adjournments again and again. We often play stuff from the sixties, seventies, and eighties, old Cuban hits, the Haitians Coupé Cloué, Francis Bebey, or the latest Nat King Cole.

Only yesterday, we met a young Frenchman doing his military service by working abroad in the Coopération, a Corsican from Porto-Vecchio he had us know, who intends to introduce us to the marvels of jazz. With jazz, through the intermediary of a beautiful Steinway piano, he claims we're achieving the democratic ideal so lacking in this country. That jazz ideal is quite simply the emergence of a full, whole individual voice in the heart of a collective voice. We applauded him loudly; we're giving ourselves a few more years to taste and restore the marvels the maestros of jazz have accumulated.

In this cloistered country, we know how, yes! we know how to listen to the melodies of the sea, drink the light, open wide our hearts and eardrums. The goal of all that is to wash the intrigues, rumors, and other nauseating machinations from our fans' ears. We know how to play the kind of music that dives double-quick into heady bass notes, slips into the meanders of our lead singer's voice, ricochets off the volcanic hills, crosses the Formica seas, dances on the edge of the horizon accompanied by an Affar flute, runs through all of this crushed land, sobs sometimes, alternates onomatopoeias and meaningful lines—putting off till tomorrow the dialectic between business and art—pleases the ear, blurs the eye, and transforms faces to reaffirm spiritual joy through song. One day soon we will succeed in fulfilling our dream: to develop a musical preface to this country in gestation, to herald the time when brand-new knowledge will suddenly burst into bloom. Somehow build a community rooted in the back country of our birth, something

like a Rasta retreat camp, an anarchist phalanstery of the kind
that existed in 1936 Spain, a pioneer kibbutz, a camp of Zapatis-
tas, a Sufi hermitage, a bivouac under the stars, a Robinson
Crusoe island, a cybercafe for immigrants connected to the old
country, an Abyssinian monastery like the one near Lalibela,
a kraal of Zulu warriors. In short, something unimaginable in
the country of our fathers. We will live as rebels, not far from
the muffled sound of arms because of this state of neither war
nor peace, neither crime nor punishment, neither head nor tail.
Perhaps you think we're going off the deep end and abandoning our roots. You are quite mistaken: we're the first band—
and the only one to this day—to sing in every language of this
place at the same time, and even in the same song, the same
breath. We are condemned to bring together all the daughters
and sons of Adam, to shed the water of our own sweat to taste
the sweat of others, to trade our tears, our saliva, and our rising
sap. To unstrap the packsaddle of ignorance that hobbles our
fellow countrymen. Believe it or not, we're on the right path,
even if it is full of stones. In every village, from north to south
and east to west, we're at home everywhere, welcomed warmly
everywhere, at ease everywhere, like those iguanas taking the
morning sun. As it was in the first days of independence. Our
emblem is the tortoise with its repulsive face and age-old wisdom, in contrast to the indolence and emptiness of man. We
take over old tunes from history books and make them ours
and new again, brilliant and shiny like a four-wheel drive Pajero
loaded with options imported from Saudi Arabia. We sample
pieces from colonial memory, like this poem from a bard who's
both French and Uruguayan:

> In Djibouti it's so hot,
> Metallic, bitter, brutal,
> They grow palm trees of metal
> The others die on the spot.

You sit beneath the scrap iron
While, grinding in the desert breeze
They pile up to your very knees,
the iron filings.

But under palms that sound like trains
Luckily, inside your brain
You're free to fantasize
A trip worldwide.

To think we nearly called ourselves Hadji Dideh, from the name of the man who signed the agreement with the French when they wanted to settle on this coast! Mau-Mau, that name down from Mount Kilimanjaro, was ideal. Two birds with one stone. First of all we can take it easy, no one's going to say we're pro-Walal, pro-Wadag, or who knows what kind of crap they can come up with. Second, it's a fighter's name, inspired by the spirits of the Kenyan forest. An anti-colonialist, anti-imperialist, Third Worldist warrior, and Pan-African to boot. It's revolutionary. Basta. *No pasaran.* It's Rasta, see. We can sing with the great I Jah Man "I Man a Warrior." Go, youth! *Avanti la musica.*

The Théâtre des Salines, which was born well before I was, has the feel of an amphitheater with its stage almost square and its terraced rows of seats looking out on the port. They used to show the films of Laurel and Hardy, the adventures of Charlie Chaplin (and so a whole bunch of neighborhood kids were nicknamed Charlie either because of their duck walk or their dreamy look, and I do know a few), and films about the exploits of Pelé (the same goes for the nickname of guys who were really good with a soccer ball). Children of the poor who'd been ignored by the Republic also got their education there, and they found nothing better to do than jump the wall and infuriate the three or four policemen sent after them from the barracks. Down below are the famous salt fields that gave the theater its name, but alas alas the salt miners of the Territory who used to break their backs for a slave's salary disappeared after the parent company, Les Salins du Midi, decided to consolidate in the south of France. A neighborhood with clean housing, Einguela, was built toward the turn of the seventies over a large part of the once muddy terrain abandoned by the company from Marseilles. The capital grew considerably larger during those years, and all the empty spaces, all the oasis-like hollows, all the places in cemeteries where dusty ancestors were still lying, all the crossroads where caravans were used to kneeling got covered with cement and lampposts. Now the eyes of the city are like moving seaweed. The Théâtre des Salines is where we play for the working people of the neighborhoods.

20

ALICE

WHEN I MET YOUR FATHER, I wasn't looking for some mythical Africa; I wasn't looking for the love of my life, the way others run after a great novelist. To tell you the truth, I wasn't looking for anything at all; I was just dragging myself around, bored and daydreaming away on the banks of the Vilaine River. Africa would come to me all by herself, like a big girl. Alas, my little cactus, it was not the rebellious continent, just the Africa of news reports as they're filtered through the clear conscience of the West. Then it became the Africa of dictators with Swiss bank accounts, the Africa of rickety children and bony old men, the Africa of famine and the shameless looting of its resources, the Africa of squalid huts and gleaming white teeth, the Africa of landless people, the Africa of guerrillas and desperados. The so-called experts who speak about Africa do not think it necessary to know its languages. Can you imagine a Sinologist who can't say hello-goodbye in the language of his studies? But I'm getting off my topic.

At that time, especially at that age, I was constantly fuming with rage, living on a volcano of passions. I wrapped up my studies of history with a college degree, and, disgusted by what they were teaching me about Africa and the French Empire, I registered for the entry examination to the School of Journalism in Paris. I felt ready to land on the burning banks of the Red Sea and examine the Africa I had begun to imagine, a many-layered, historical pastry with unique sedimentation. Your father joined me there, abandoning his band of friends with a heavy heart. He seemed to have grown up: in a few weeks, he had climbed the steps of age it usually takes many years to ascend. The perspective of finding his country still under colonial rule had given him wings, even if he dreaded the ordinary racism on both sides of the fence and what people might say once we were settled there. He lived through the last months of his life in Paris like a passerby, light-heartedly wearing the first wrinkles on his brow and a little paunch in his midsection. He couldn't care less about it, because in Djibouti, when you're married and past thirty, people talk to you like you're a responsible man, the head of a family, an almost-old man. Then, very quickly, came the whirlwind of the return. For the first few months, you don't really know who you are. You go from one house to another, one family to another, one friend to another with the assurance of a tightrope walker. You listen to advice; you collect various views and contradictory opinions with the same ears, without asking yourself too many questions. You don't really know who you are, or who they are. Everything is intoxicating: visiting the country, combing the city. Real life, right? But that feeling won't last. Soon, they put you in a ready-made box: you're the mixed couple people look at suspiciously. On lonely evenings (or their corollary, boring ones), you'll catch yourself sobbing at the prospect of once again having to face the gaping sadness that comes after dusk. You tell yourself that for him, you're ready to accept pain, humiliation, and even the sorrow to come, when things become normal, when his family wants to take back their man. We'll be caught in the midst of the storm, but alive and strong. In that situation of insidious adversity, you can only get tougher. A little inner voice would whisper to me on difficult days: "What made you come here to this land of echoes and dust, this antechamber of the desert where they bury the dead quickly to prevent the flies from gathering and performing their diabolical ballet? You're breathing an air made of boredom, routine, and triumphant poverty. Here, no one's going to ask much of you. Where will you put your tombstone if anything happened to you? Let this man and people like him soliloquize till the end of time."

A month after our arrival, both of us found work. The authorities must have wanted to polish up their image: a domino couple with college degrees just off the plane, isn't exactly run-of-the-mill here, even if the president of the territorial council, M. Ali Aref, dug up a Frenchwoman from Nîmes—a naive lady, they say—with the help of Jacques Foccart, the man who distributes destinies in French-speaking countries allied with France. In September 1973, I was starting my first year of teaching at the Boulaos junior high school and your father joined the little scientific institute mainly devoted to geology, which had just opened its doors on the road to the airport. I really couldn't bring myself to be a journalist under the "leadership" of the high commissioner of the Republic, and aside from reporting on sports scores, I don't see what I could have shared with this milieu. I remained walled up in my silence with my colleagues; almost all of them were French, spurred on by the prospect of buying their rented apartment in a few months. Open my heart to them—are you kidding? They would have thought I was crazy, a terrorist almost, a half-wit who should be sent back on the first ship bound for France. I could read hypocrisy, spinelessness, and cowardice in their eyes. I kept my distance, never letting them think their meaningful glances or invitations had any effect on me.

Stay on your own side of the river, and above all never throw oil on the fire, never arouse the right-wing crowds of the colony and pet the muzzle of Lucifer. At first, we managed to avoid the cold kiss of killing steel by keeping ourselves at a respectful distance from the authorities. But as one might expect—and perhaps we nourished some illusions in this respect—your father received a cool welcome from his family, and even from some of his friends who had recently returned to the fold. The time was not ripe for mixed-race love or mixed flavors in this erratic country, this womb so fertile it cannot keep its children unless it uses a straitjacket and holds them in neurotic silence.

When we landed we were dreaming of a world in which people looked each other straight in the eye and spoke to each other like human beings, a world where people spoke man to man the way South Americans address each other—*Hombre!*—with no distinctions of class, race, or nationality. Alas, this country and its sun drove me mad. Their way of living in apnea infuriated me. Always waiting, spying on the neighbor's breathing, the cousin's breathing, the breathing of the man who came back from Ethiopia that summer or the woman who just found a meaningless administrative job at the Fisheries through her relatives. Waiting. Waiting. I could have written a whole notebook of his return to the country of his ancestors as I waited.

But there were also things more serious than my petty bouts of melancholy; what's more, you know me, I'm not a poetess of the tropics, you can see that straightaway, right? Sure, they'd warned me, but really, as long as you haven't lived through something yourself it's a waste of time. As long as you haven't felt the tough, concrete reality in your own flesh it doesn't amount to a row of beans. Ali Aref's henchmen kept the little colony in a state of permanent terror as if their political mentors were Dr. Malan and the farmer Ian Smith, respectively the brain behind apartheid in South Africa and the strong man

of the future Zimbabwe, then called Southern Rhodesia after
the name of the British explorer and builder but nonetheless
exterminator Cecil Rhodes. On the map of Africa, only Djibouti—besides Rhodesia and Pretoria—was still living under
the colonial yoke. I'm sorry, my little cactus, if I'm giving you
so many political examples that are not from your time. It's to
better render the sound and fury of that period, nauseating
and explosive all at once, and then I felt terrible when they as-
sociated me with the last little bunch of colonists just because
I was French. In fact, I was a walking disgrace; maybe you'll
understand that some day. An animal with horns avoided by
your father's so-called friends. I couldn't have cared less about
their distrust, aside from the fact that all around us the atmo-
sphere was insurrectional. The lower city was untenable even
if the Foreign Legion held the main roads and intersections
from the end of the afternoon on. On the Richter scale of fear,
our world had toppled into eruptive, telluric panic. A world the
color of meat and blood. Of poverty, too: never had I seen so
many begging hands at every bus stop, so many malnourished
children as there were the month after we arrived. It's because
of the famine in Ethiopia, said the propaganda. And a world
of bling and lucre, where, at noon prayer on Fridays, we could
already see crowds of SUVs, exhibited as zebus once were in
times gone by.

Ali Aref and his supporters had done all they could to sort
people out, and anathema and exclusion were the rule. Your
membership in a tribe, or more precisely a clan, contrary to
the common appellation, was stamped on your identity card,
and, as if that weren't enough, they invented a new population category, decreed non-native on the pretext that they were
supposed to be from Somalia. Non-natives and nomads of the
inner country had to go through the Balbala checkpoint to get
here, to the capital. This checkpoint was a miniature Berlin

Wall. One word too many and you'd be accused of sabotage on the spot, handcuffed, shackled, and brought to the Service du Fichier, the data agency behind the only high school in the colony—attended mainly by children of expats, let me say in passing. You had two solutions: confess all the sins of Israel and you had a very slight chance of being released, broken but alive, intellectually annihilated but still hanging onto life by the guardrail. You would return home, but it was an open secret that you'd been turned; appointed by the secret services and their slave forever, you'd be constantly on edge now: you'd take to your heels at the sight of a dead caterpillar. The other solution: you had nothing to confess, had committed no crime, and your corpse would be carried by the tide between Haramouss and Loyada or, at two cable-lengths from town, between the slaughterhouses and Boulaos, half-decapitated by a shark, twisting in a net of seaweed, your skin eaten away by salt and the sun of the Last Judgment as an eyewitness. Of course there were a few exceptions, widely bruited about and held up as examples to hail the kind indulgence of the white chief. Again and again they told of the case of such-and-such, a young man from a good family led into the temptation of rebellion, the harmful influence of friends quickly detected, the virus eradicated, the young man miraculously saved from deadly waters, God recognizing his own, God always works in mysterious ways with resurrection at the end of the road, blah-blah-blah, once he was put on the straight and narrow the young man was sent off to study in France with a scholarship awarded by the Territory like that Vic Lebleu and his silly nickname.

Despite battalions of paid informers, the wrath of the people never ceased to explode during the two decades of the Aref regime. The people found a way to express itself creatively, each link in the chain doing its job; with no clear leader, the results

were obvious nonetheless: now the people was building bar-
ricades in poor neighborhoods, driving the Legionnaires away
with stones, occupying Gabode prison, derailing trains, boy-
cotting French products and schools, and refusing to pay taxes
of all kinds, as in August 1966. Everything would suddenly calm
down for a while, and then, without advance notice, start up
again with renewed vigor. The staccato drone of helicopters
grazing the rooftops and the heads of the demonstrators, the
suffocating smell of tear gas, the neighborhoods locked down,
the main roads blocked, the headquarters of the labor unions
sacked, the arbitrary arrests, lashes of whips, pointless humili-
ations, expulsions from the country, the corpses of activists
on the sidewalks—everything was catching fire again. Then
back to calm. The cycle of struggles would begin its rounds
again elsewhere, tomorrow, based on spontaneous anger, underground activism, the slogans of poets and singers, the ruses
of the multitude—the thousand-and-one faces of solidarity.
The multitude is the old woman who carries in water to soothe
eyes smarting from the gas; it is the women who gather stones
and give them to the men and to the children who have taken
the vanguard—*mater dolorosas* and amazons all at once. The
multitude is the muezzin who calls for insubordination and at
the same time for prayer and return to the bosom of God. The
multitude is the rage of the rebels, most often adolescents, con-
fronting forces stronger than they are, biting the dust and getting up again to charge the enemy. The multitude is repetition,
too. Starting again, always. Resistance and desire are present
in every moment of life. Raising an old bush song to rally, relay,
reconnect, wake sleeping energy, shake the genealogical tree.
The old underground laws show the tip of their nose. Raids,
razzias, fantasias, vendettas, last-ditch stands, everything that
could frighten the good organization of the colony. Depriving
the high commissioner of sleep, and his local native, too. Tell-

ing the outside world, seeking out potential allies in the enemy camp. It is impossible for the police to contain the movement, its life, its protuberances, its transformations, its desires and its new needs, which come from afar, from very far. Silence, exile, and cunning. Crossing and re-crossing borders that make no sense for anyone; a surge of nomadic life, mobility, cooperation, exchange, sharing, the power to annoy. "Irredentism, irredentism," shouted the head of the high commissioner's cabinet. No matter.

Protect oneself from stupidity. The savor of being and existing. Tactical retreat and return to the source. Going back to square one, to your mental hinterland—something larger than this colony the size of a postage stamp or a piece of dust-covered confetti. Ah, the great day was approaching. You could feel it in the air. You could feel it because morale on the other side was at a low point. All beginnings are lyrical; what follows, not so much. There was lyricism and carnival in that resistance. You could sense a huge dynamic force capable of propelling destiny forward. This rabble was stealthily bringing the French Republic under Pompidou to the court of universal conscience in the name of Republican values.

21

ABDO-JULIEN

"IN THE MIDST of the forests and savannahs and ergs, in the red burning embers of the cities above the wild sea, on the sweet-smelling hills where the butterflies play, there lived a beautiful beast, warm and tawny, which was called happiness." *Dixit* the Breton storyteller Maria Kermadec, who often concludes her ramblings with a proverb she attributes to a sailor from Cancale: "He who has words in his mouth can never get lost in the world."

Maman's records, old vinyls buckled by the heat, rarely leave their pink candy jackets these days. If the hippie queens, the hepcat princes, Janis Joplin and Jimi Hendrix, Marianne Faithfull, and French singers like Brigitte Fontaine, Georges Moustaki, Barbara (her favorite), remain silent, prisoners stuck in their plastic covers, it's because Maman's sunny disposition has been stymied. As for Papa, his shelf of records is drawn from the rugged paradise of Deep South blues: Sonny Boy Williamson, Muddy Waters, and Bobby Bland share his favors. To make him reel into nostalgia, no need for khat. Otis Redding, Marvin Gaye, and Smokey Robinson remain his youth pills. Maman needs a particular microclimate to open that magic box. Old friends coming over, a phone call from an old girl-friend from Rennes, a bunch of youthful memories, things like that. Something still simpler: a melody, an old hit heard on the radio during a short trip, and you can be sure Maman's going to dust off the record player and play her twenty-odd LP records and as many 45s one by one. The whole household will be invaded by the brash voices of artists belting out all the music they have in them. In general, it goes in cycles and can easily take three to four days. The music of their youth has a beneficial effect on the morale of the troops: Papa perks up, even tries a few dance steps, imitating a matador with his sharp pin; Maman is jovial at first, then suddenly the tension mounts and swings into hysteria once the needle has landed on a Janis Joplin record. That's who she's imitating now. And all this can end in a terrible noise of broken dishes. No two ways about it, she's howling like a hangman at confession. The neighbors are taken aback for a while, wondering if everything's OK in the family of Harbi Awaleh and Alice, the daughter of the Breton storyteller who used to collect old ten-centime colonial stamps—"Madagascar and Dependencies"—and Abdo-Julien, that's me, stillborn in his seventeenth year, spirit wandering in the great tradition of the dibbuks you can find in *The Golem*, a small child returning periodically like the *abikou** in the region of the Gulf of Guinea whose umbilical cord is buried next to Ilé-Ifé—an extraordinary fate, in the direct line of the *shafeec** of our people. I owe everything I know to my parents. Does that surprise you?

22

BASHIR BINLADEN

WAR INTO OVERTIME on the field now. President brought
in a lot-lot draftees to replace all the dead. And then Scud 2,
it start talking negotiations. The chiefs went quick-quick into
town to get armchairs, A/Cs an radios. Ran like rabbits to pick
up armchairs before their friends. Chiefs of Scud-there, they
so-so hungry they'd eat their rebel boots. President so happy,
he decorated the wounded, soldiers without arms, soldiers
without legs, children without papa an mama. He accepted
wounded rebels in big hospital to make buddy-buddy with sec-
ond-in-command of Eternal Opponent. So it real peace now.
Cept Eternal Opponent left for Paris to take refuge, he said
war-there not over, said Scud 2 sold out corrupt. Him, watch
out he gonna throw Scud 3 onto the field now.

Hey, that true truth cause ambush start again at Randa, Am-
bado, As-Dara, an all. So us we stay stuck in military positions
at Dikhil, Tadjoura, Obock, an in the Mabla. We defensive
forwards to save the sovereignty and gains of the united and
indivisible nation, that fat rich language like French head of
diplomacy talk. So all that-there, not too bad for us, right? Me,
that's how I kept my job. All the guys relax; we have fun after

we cried a lot cause of buddies dead on the sideline like Hous-
seini in Adaylou, the one who bought and sold the pink pills.
Everybody knows the pills-there come direct from Mogadishu; they love pills there too much so they can keep on with
fierce war. Normal, right? But you can't make fun of the other
monkey's cunt when your own ass-there naked too, even. Somalians, they in deep shit, but we got our problems too. The
whole world saying: Somalians, Africans, all a bunch of sav-
ages make civil war all the time. Well, gotta understand us.
What you expect when politicians-there they pick up all the
pots an chow? When they eat the skin off the nape-a your neck.
You pick up rifle, that's all. Us, we don't got comfort, villa, car,
pay vacation like French, English, an even Norwegians who're
nice cause they give NGO money an keep their trap shut. Me
I say if a big white guy he wanna take my place, I give it right
away an go screw his wife an daughter. That way it democracy
between us. I give my place an he take my place here. Then I
take his wife. Tie, ball in midfield. Be serious now and stop
that crap about rightsaman, rightsawoman, rightsababies. We
got a right to the good life too, don't we? Sick of drinking our
own sweat. Draftees wanna admire shooting stars too, cept
what they see's tracer bullets singing sweet little songs like this:
"C'mere my little honey, come this way, been waiting for you for
a long long time." Draftees, they like that old camel the family
gonna kill to eat him cause he's too-too old. The old camel, he
say to chief of camp: "I worked for you all my life. I marched,
marched, and marched to carry your tent and your merchandise. You got all you needed out of my back, now you wanna
eat my meat and bones. After that you still get more out of me
cause you'll take my skin an you'll make shoes with it, right?"
So there you are, us draftees like ole camel-there cept us, we
younger. That's all. Gotta stop bringing tears to my eyes. I close
parenthesis.

Now on the field there not only Scud 3 but also NGO who wanna help rebels by giving medicine, OK with me, but also LAV (that mean light armored vehicle) an bazookas. Me, I say no fair. OK, NGO can help rebels a little but come on, gotta help us a little too. That way it justice. You give grub to one brother, gotta give grub to other one. Me, I think business-there a little not clear. NGO, they say we gonna give grub to population, but behind they making strong allies. We caught an old white woman hiding boxes of Chinese grenades in her white truck with blue flag. So President, he get real mad, bang on his desk, yell: I don't wanna see no more NGO humanimajig on the field. You catch one, you kill him right there. I will personally send a bill to the main office of his organization for the bullet he gets between the eyes. From now on, these people will be carrying their coffins on their backs. Now me, that where I say, bravo. Big bravo even. Can see he not kidding around no more, the ole president. That crystal clear like the desert sky.

23

ALICE

AT THE VERY BEGINNING of the seventies, Abdouwahid Egueh, aka Vic Lebleu, aka Victor or more commonly the Guy from Lille because he almost became the first soccer player of the Territory sent to France, had only played two seasons for the club of the big northern city, which was then in the Second Division. Perseverance was not his strong point, so he came back home in secret. Needless to say, Wahid, the Unique, was not up to the hopes that had been placed on him. However, between Lille and him there was a wild love story, at least at the start. But that wasn't all: his trip to the other world gave him a laid-back attitude that became legendary. Vic Lebleu is a new man now, blathering away on Triton Beach night and day, spending most of his time on Plateau du Héron, neglecting the family house in District 4. A gang leader with no other authority than his good humor, he hangs around with Chiné (the Chinese, a little thug) and his friends, killing time in front of the Clochard (Tramp) Stand, a stone's throw from the Olympia cinema. He brags about his ability to move effortlessly through all social milieus—not just the expatriates he's after all year long—and speaks, in addition to his French peppered with swearwords and Lille slang, the three languages currently used in this part of the world. Late at night, Vic and Chiné's whole gang meet at the Mic-Mac, a shady spot but very popular in the capital, something between a dance hall, a nightclub, and a hangout for whores. On the dance floor Vic wiggles his hips, with honeyed eyes and catlike steps. With his laughs, ramblings, and easy gab, he's the king of the dance floor, a pasha reigning over his little sultanate, Sinbad sailing between the scent of tobacco and hops. And yet a perceptive eye will probably sense his vulnerability. Very grave things are said about him. He's said to be an agent provocateur in the pay of the secret services. When he got back from Lille he was taken over by very sure hands. If you wanted to take the trouble to look for his umbilical cord, you'd find it around District 4 or Einguela. His almost perfect knowledge of the field is not something to be overlooked in these uncertain times. His encyclopedic cackling about the underworld, marked by what he has skimmed from rumors, can be useful. Ferdinand Valombreuse, Aref's shadowy right-hand man and an expert in dirty work, ran into him a few times in the officers' mess hall on Boulevard de Gaulle and can attest to it. They looked each other up and down for a long time. In the soft languor of a muggy afternoon, they clinked their glasses of Heineken together. Vic's face took on an auriferous glow, and Valombreuse, with a 180-degree smile, left the premises to go about the business he had set for himself that day.

The first mission they gave Vic was child's play. He had to find two or three house painters and whitewash the blood-covered walls of the Teacher Training College after the student revolt mentioned above. Once the work was over, he would leave his usual signature or more exactly his initials (VL for Vic Lebleu) in the corner of one of the walls, the way a Renaissance painter might sign his stained glass windows. More prosaically, this signature is a cabbalistic sign for men in the secret services.

Vic joined their stable at an early age. He admired their crafty style and above all flipped at their risky games and their taste for bling-bling. You can easily follow their route at regular times in the upper city. Omar Bashé and Gourmad Robleh, the excellent sleuths on the vice squad fresh from police school at the École Nationale in Villeurbanne do exactly that, but discreetly. Towards four PM they leave Triton Beach. At five, they have sodas and cans of beer in a dark bar run by an Ethiopian ex-prostitute. The hand moves around the clock once more and they're taking the air near the industrial port, opposite the Coca-Cola bottling plant. At eight, they're strolling along the coast road, built at the exact spot of the present Route de Venise (a gift from Italian Cooperation) always two by two, three hundred yards apart from each other, stopping to smoke a cigarette, quicken their step or on the contrary slow down. They pass by soldiers in tracksuits trotting along on their way back to the naval base on Heron Island. The draftees, noisier than a kindergarten hive, don't hesitate to provoke them from a distance. All winks, chuckles, and sighs. Vehicles with the insignia of Air Detachment 188 slow down as they reach the swampy zone. Stares coming from all sides, coupled with little nervous laughs. The mares waddle along, let themselves be desired. A new moon shiny as a twenty-franc piece is beginning to glimmer in the coal-black sky. From time to time, the headlights of a civilian car shoot out of the bottleneck of the port; the mares slow down and make themselves very visible on the sidewalk under the halo of the lampposts. Playing at innocent games, they suck a Miko ice cream bar they'd bought previously or lick a cone, their faces turned towards the peaceful sound of the sea.

24

AWALEH

THE TREE OF NIGHT grows in secret. It sees its shadow getting longer or shorter and swallows the day and the night in one gulp. The traveler tree relieves man from the scorching heat of summer—a veritable open-air hammam. The tree of the monsoon turns itself into a vaporizer, an atomizer; the spirits of the ancestors weave hosannas for it to add to its laurels. The palm tree of the city gives a bit of shade to the white uniforms staggering around Place Menelik at noon. Happy today as it was yesterday, the mangrove tree takes under its wing mud crabs, leeches, and knotty eels. The ocean tree protects madrepores, sponges beneath the swell, and moving corals—a whole maritime orchestra. Here, the earth, too, writes history, with its aftershakes, its down-strokes and up-strokes, and its bubbling slaver. The madrepore reefs are the tales told by the sea and by an omniscient sun. The mountain tree, you'll find it farther north. The tree of the dried-up wadi lashes your face. The tree of the stony field flecks the flint-colored landscape with touches of green. The tree of the wind, pilgrim of the hills, turns right, turns left. The tree of the sands will smile under your soles if you're willing to pay attention to it. We use the dung of cows and the earth of anthills to fertilize the fields, and the song of the moon trees rises from them, did you know that, my boy? The dwarf tree of the undergrowth saved the life of the mythical Accompong, the runaway Jamaican slave still alive in the heart of the Rastafarians. (*Are you a slave? No, I am an Ethiopian. Down with Babylon! Hail Haile Selassie!*—a Rasta with super-thick hair and a mellifluous voice, a dubber, as you hummed to me only yesterday, my seraphic grandson. I was wondering where you get all that stuff.) The generation tree par excellence, more than the lantana, is the banyan, of course. The tree of your placenta, the womb of your being, the embryo of your future history, is safely buried in the courtyard of the house. And the little tree of memory, can you guess? The cactus. That's you, my little cactus.

25

BASHIR BINLADEN

NOW I GOT BAD NEWS, too-too bad, dunno if I should blurt it out in front of everybody. Scud 3, it took back more positions, As-Eyla, Bolli, Ripta, Weima, an all. So us, we use a lot of helicopters for supplies cause rebellion has good field position. Day, Goda, Mabla, all that, it mountain an mountain. Score: 1–0 rebellion, you got me? But OK, all that, it not too serious. One day win for goverment, tomorrow for rebellion. All that same an one, man. French referee, he watched game from sideline. Everybody said loud: you help him an not me. So you, you get out of minefield fast or watch your white ass-there. Referee he got out quick-quick with dumb moron smile on his face an look of someone who grazed too much. He went hide in French Consulate. From there he gonna yell funny dirty words: summary executions, torture, rape, arbitrary arrest, child soldiers, pogroms (that word weird, seem not too-too French), purges, barbarous practices, massacres, ethnic cleansing, etc. His language-there too funny; sounds like medicines. Doctor or referee, gotta choose. Who cares; he gone now. Good for him, he in safe place now, cause on the field, stray bullet come in real fast.

So, the too-too bad news you trying to find it, right? No, not
Scud 3 just won battle of Assagueila. No no, not white coward
referee either. The not-so-nice news, it's our friends demobilized. You forgot demobilized draftees already or what? That
demobilization business don't work right cause goverment refuse to give money to guys not in uniform no more. It don't
refuse right out but play for time too much, you know, like when
Brazilians ahead 3–0 fifteen minutes before end of game. Before that demobilization business, there was that displacement
thing, really made soldiers head too-too hot. Lot of demobilized guys don't have feet, legs, hands an walk on their ass. So-
so pitiful for veteran who used to run fast, used to kill fast like
Bruce Lee an drill young gazelles. Our demobilized friends,
they real mad, normal, right? So, they attacked headquarters
with grenades in their pockets. Maximum scandal in Djibouti
town. Old president, he got too scared of coup. Motherfucka.
The army, it attacked demobilized guys on strike and killed ten
an ten just like that, in Balbala and District 7b. *Wallahi!* Too
unfair cause when army can't control territory, it say to mobilized guys: help me help me, and now it kills little demobilized
guys asking for their money. Next time, it gonna be our turn.
Gotta prepare with morale of ferocious fighter. This time our
friends lost KO but next time we can win on points. Now, the
city shameless, they calling demobilized guys deserters. Hey,
you heard that with your big fat ears, my deserter friends. Dis-
gustation force five, I say. City lost its head or what, or the old
president the one off his rocker now. World assy-turvy. Fuck
you, deserters yourself. Next time, gonna be our turn. And
then, it gonna get hot. I'm gonna put on King Kong voice, deep
an fiery. Take it from Binladen who does his five prayers and
screws the Americans standing up.

26

ALICE

THE PENCIL OF LIGHT from the Balbala lighthouse will show you the road as soon as you cross the Ambouli wadi. Even if the night is pitch black, all you have to do is follow the intermittent beams from the beacon and, in the intervals, avoid the ruts in the road—no easy business. You'll rush into your concession and there will surely be a lot of people sleeping already, some of them snoring, others wriggling around on narrow mats, trying to find the sleep that eludes them after one hell of a khat party. Others rolled up on themselves like Labradors. Still others squeezed together shoulder to shoulder in rows, praying in a makeshift mosque. Once you're in your shack, you'll stretch out on your bed—"stretch out" is too big a word for a reduced-size bed more like a hammock than a tatami due to its worn-out springs on a base thin as a piece of cigarette paper—and finally you'll collapse. Sleep won't come right away, nor in the first hour, and you'll watch the film of your day in half-hour batches. You'll break down every action, every event. Nothing interesting to get from it, your life being what it is. You'll count sheep; you'll have plenty of time to try and catch the fleeing night. You'll raise your eyes toward the migrating stars. You'll imagine yourself traveling on the rump of a dromedary, arriving in mysterious Timbuktu, unless it's Palmyra and the surrounding desert. It's no good. Soon it will be day outside. The beam of the beacon will end its round. You'll get up, but not quite yet, waiting until your eyes can get rid of the surrounding darkness. Your willpower will sputter out like a candle, your muscles in disarray, your spine turning to jelly. All your efforts will be reduced to neon dust by an invisible force, a force you'll feel hiding there inside yourself, cutting away your efforts, undermining your spurts of energy. You'll feel your legs with your fingers, like someone trying to feel the pain in a phantom limb. Your legs are there, hooked up to your trunk, but they won't obey you. It will feel as if you're trying to size up the height, depth, and volume of your imprisonment. Desire is there, but not motion. You recognize your physical state as one of those déjà-vu feelings typical of sleepless nights. Is that what's called the *douboab*, the genie that's been let out of the bottle on a day without khat? Who knows. A new day is awaiting you, exactly the same as the day before. And that's not something to be happy about.

Why are you looking at me with that dumb smile? I'm not good at telling stories, or what? Let me tell you this, my little man. When you tell a story, listen to me my love my rosebud my first picture book, yes, when you release the flow of a story, everything depends on the connection between the parts, the way one sequence fits into another, the sudden eruption of chance and the proper use of the catalogue and the series. The most natural order is rarely apparent immediately. It takes shape through detours, approximations, and the compass of ellipses—in other words through renewed repetitions. The narrative voices push and shove each other, and you have to capture the force that drives them, that's all. Chewing-digesting, cutting-and-pasting will sometimes do the trick. You can't neglect the humble details: isn't it true that Alpine torrents originate from a thin little brooklet and the tumultuous waters of the Nile from a kind of marsh in the depths of Burundi? Nor can you forget that no matter how small we are on this world here below, our heart keeps beating along with the distant stars. We are born star-fishers, and there's nothing to be done about it. Our body, connecting and amalgamating the infinitely far and the immediately near, loses, as it does so, a reserve of energy and strength. Our faith remains indestructible, as if it were made of bricks and silence, far from the encumberment of language and far from those who are still sitting inside what has been forgotten, sunk in silence. In the world of your little mothers (your aunts in the language of this country), they say that the shape of a head often shows what kind of daydreams, fantasies, and plans take place inside it. Is this true, or an illusion? I know all kinds of noggins, and I couldn't be so categorical about it: some people even have a head for two. They're called lunatics, and the flowers of their mind are scattered over many worlds and various skies. There are brains that are smothered and suffer from the overpopulation of gloomy thoughts; others remain forever becalmed (as they say in Brittany of a flat sea), empty and unpopulated. Incongruity, freshness, or accuracy of the image—you decide. There are heads that love the jousting of muscles and curves, the *awele* of words thrown to the four winds, all the way to the Country of the Celestial Dragon (China in the language of our country, the French of France even for me, half Breton). Heads in fezzes that set out to collect every little event of the sand country. There are seekers of Africas, hunters of quickly gathered evidence. Other guys with hope between their teeth and an empty belly. Stories passed around forever actually save their lives, bring them out of the social coma, pump some vigorous blood into their vegetating body. So they enter into books and stories as into a pyramid. Our men's destiny is not sustained by social muscles or industrial revolutions but by trading in dreams, by the imagination. At night, once they have gone through the gate of tears, they bump into the door of the sun. But far off, very far off is the cape of hope with its heavenly scents, victuals galore, and constant banquets, its salads of fruit, its streams of milk and honey, its bay-leaf soaps, its lotions for all ills, its forest of aphrodisiac bois bandé, its undergrowth of trails, its climbing ivy, virgin vines, generous olive trees, its royal palm trees heavy with dates, its deceptive brambles that welcome the young martyrs who hurled themselves valiantly into death, its Scottish thistles, its South Sea aromas, its rising mountains, its soft, fluid, fragrant fountains of youth, the abracadabra of its pleasures. But I'm getting you all mixed up, I know. I'm sorry.

27

ABDO-JULIEN

PAPA'S FACE HAS SOMETHING troubling and fragile in it, something he owes to his years of famine and anguish, something that comes from way back, from his childhood I imagine; the attraction of nothingness is visible in his eyes, too. Every evening, his account of what was really a rather banal day has sounded strange to our ears recently. The words, first of all: words of a hounded man, of a wounded soul. And then the tone: a tone of elegy. One silently wonders how much oxygen is left in this tall, reserved man. Most people around here respect him a great deal, and he's head and shoulders above those who ignore him. People from all walks of life come to our house: Blacks and Whites, browns like me, the nobodies of the day and the phantoms of the night. Opponents of the regime who slip in stealthily. Reciters of 114 suras of the holy Book. He listens to their complaints and dips into his pocket more often than he should.

Ancestors also move surreptitiously around our home at sunset. Spirits who live with us: we can sense them crossing the courtyard at set times; a little whirlwind of sand follows them. Sometimes we breathe in their smell hours after they've gone by; we can also hear their clicking, and Papa announces that they, too, are beginning their day of cooking and household chores. No need to be in on the secret; all you have to do is perk up your ears and open wide your eyes. Nor do you need the strength of the cart-pullers you can see on Place Rimbaud to stand up to those spirits: they're quite peaceful and avoid us, because we're the ones who have remained blind, unable to see them coming. It is said that they go to great lengths not to crush us like eggshells. Unless you have the bad luck to surprise them, but then all they do is slap you—which may well send you straightaway into the other world. So many of us are found at dawn with frightened eyes, bewildered minds, and drool at the corner of the lips. A sheikh or a djinn-hunter is called to the rescue. Someone who can do nothing, or just about, most of the time. And the unfortunate victim drags himself around on his bottom every day, or never leaves his bed again. His life will be nothing but misery and survival, between rats and garbage. A stench that almost makes you faint.

Speaking of rats, they say they graze on you in your sleep; you can feel them walking over you. The boldest ones nibble the rough skin of your feet and breathe on the exact spot they just bit as if to soothe you or keep you asleep. If you sleep without any light—and worse, with no mosquito netting—watch out for your toes; they can bite you bloody. If you're exasperated by the squeaks of these rodents or the whirring of bat wings, don't try to kill them; the ancestors have forbidden it. They have been blood relations for eternities. Outside, only the gleam of braziers or storm-lamps and the sounds of people clearing their throats give life to the alleys. The best you can do is leave the muddy days on the tip of your toes, wait for dawn, and pray to the Ancients. Only children, boys in particular (they are considered a source of wealth comparable to the fat accumulated in a ram's tail), have some small chance of being listened to—and even then. Tomorrow we'll see if the lying, limping hyena has not carried everything away in its path. Tomorrow we'll see if the beggars can do something for the many, the very many, who have not gained favor with the spirits of the dead. Those who the ebb and flow of famine have progressively deposited in the city like alluvium in the hollow of oases. Papa used to tell a story that he got from Grandpa Awaleh, to wit: alms are given to the mystical beggars of Bengal so that the seven lotuses that sleep in each of us may blossom. A story brought back to us by the Yemenites, those Phoenicians of the Red Sea.

28

AWALEH

I, TOO, HAVE RETURNED from far away and from many dangers. I have traveled the length and breadth of the screes, deserts of sand, ergs and regs, the sides of bald mountains, and the dunes round as a dromedary's hump. I have slaked my thirst with the sap of the tamarins and aloes that grow in the beds of the wadis. A mere scrap would satisfy my hunger. Hidden in the silence of the desert, I moved like a chameleon with the slowness of a glacier. I had in my blood the required economy of breath, the uneasiness of the sentinel, and the gaze that abolishes the horizon. My companions and I—the famous Desert Scorpions that a discreet, jovial Italian friend, Hugo Pratt, had put on a saddle in his picture books, so I've been told—instinctively knew how to detect the pulsations of the earth's crust, sound the very guts of the desert, decode the book of the sands, and sense the coming of a storm. Free ourselves of whatever hampers the step, weighs down the walk, and dampens the forward thrust. The most gifted of us had the power to put the deepest song of the earth into words, wary of the small change of everyday words, a song that wells up from its belly, song of the slow crossing, a song unfolding to infinity. An opening onto the familiar world visited, lived in, questioned a thousand times. Since the beginning of time, we—that is, me and all my colleagues working in Guistir, the region of the three borders (Djibouti, Somalia, Ethiopia) that saw me born—haven't needed official documents to accompany that melody, to catch it at its birth, at the time when the cold desert night is separated from the reseda-yellow light of dawn. No member of our army of border guards, called ANG,[1] has an authentic birth certificate; we were all "born circa..." Because nomadic time is not regulated by any calendar or encumbered by any archive, it does not sign the official papers demanded by the goatees of the Third Republic. Everybody was "born circa" in my time, and only the intrusion of the French colonial administration could impose such a delicate intention on us. For our own good, of course. And we accepted it without trying to bargain. That is our strength, our pride, for we were careful not to reveal our raw, intimate thoughts to the Occupier, and as soon as things turned sour, at a sign or the snap of a finger we would take off: the whiteness, the white-hot iron bar of the sun of insubordination, was ours—the only horizon within our reach. Do not trust appearances, those old men who drag their bones to the shade of the palm tree, the ones you meet by the roadside—they keep up an exhausting pace as soon as they set their body into motion. With their nose to the wind, one foot in front of another, in the thickness of the dunes or the rough surface of the ergs—once they have set off, no one can stop them. And all those seasons with their terrifying faces, we would spend them in the nomadic backcountry. From khamsin to monsoon, we came and went between the coast and the hinterland, with some exceptional periods, like the English blockade under Churchill, which plunged the Territory, governed by

1. Autonomous Nomadic Groups.—*Author's note*

the Vichy regime with an iron hand, into the depths of hunger and thirst. During that blockade, the people of this country tasted bitter roots and cat bouillon: the memory of that time is still tattooed on them to this day.

But let us return to our old walkers, whom the administration never succeeded in taming. And how! We walked faster than the beat of their drum, we were tireless; caravan robbers know something about that. Hear this: when we were returning from a surveillance mission around Lake Abbé—"that copper sulfate-colored lake," as Hugo Pratt wrote in his little spiral notebooks—to the great astonishment of the scientists in the capital, we discovered fossils. We had noticed that after heavy rains, the soil around the lake would soften and reveal animals (small crocodiles, birds, fish, or warthogs) that had been perfectly preserved in the briny mud for eight thousand years. Not a word of thanks from the paleontologists and geologists of the capital. A fossil is an open book, I told myself. What did he tell us exactly, that dear old Hugo, about half-open books? Oh yes, he was talking about Tagore, a man from India he said was as wise as our shepherds who had the faculty of distinguishing living beings and objects under a weak light or even at night: "An open book is a talking brain; closed, a waiting friend; forgotten, a forgiving soul; destroyed, a weeping heart." Replace "book" with "earth" and you'll have some idea of the magical spells hidden in this land where man was not born of Adam but of little Lucy. These oasis landscapes always throw us into long meditative hours that Charles de Foucauld—the skeleton-thin hermit of the Hoggar, another man Hugo Pratt admired—would have appreciated. The sun of this country is a richly colored doublet; its moon is quicksilver. Its cacti bathe in a light so elegant you'd think they're filled with blue blood. The gentle pastels of its skies at the crack of dawn have in them something that can change any normally constituted person into a sensory sponge. All these spells stir in the mouths of our storytellers, those barometers of public opinion who fear the silence of the body. They're itching to explain the mysteries hidden in nature and humanity through the language of magic. The wire of a detonator lies unrolled here; you can follow its traces between the rocks. They stroke the muzzle of creation, use only ancient weapons (the stone is also a weapon, the word, the breath, the flint rubbed until it sparks; think for a moment of the bare hands imprinted on the rough cave by our distant great-grandfathers), and put a dying future in perspective by chewing over its past again and again. They suffer under our sun. They die under our moon, knowing the extreme urgency of the creative act. They are from no place. They tell time. They tell destiny.

29

BASHIR BINLADEN

GAME REALLY OVER this time. President he said OK, civil war, over. Scud 1, Scud 2, an Scud 3 said hey put it there! even if a little skinny group (Scud 4) stayed in Goda mountains with a spokeman hidden in Paris. All over for us too. War sweet as sugarcane, finished. Period. Binladen given you his word. The chiefs said: leave everything; get out right way. Clowns think it easy, like taking bus to see karate movie at the Odeon. OK, we didn't try to be wiseguys. We left quick-quick. Game ended 0–0. Tie game, OK, but hey, that business-there not zero killed. Lot of guys killed even, but that not really my problem. We took our gear, plus a few souvenirs we lifted here-an-there. We got on military truck to Camp As-Eyla then into other police truck to Ali-Sabieh, an there we got onto the roof of the old train to Djibouti. That way we travel free. To give our hands something to do, we took khat from people by force an we sung "I'm Bad" (that, American song cause Michael Jackson, he sing like he chewing big fat chewngum). We horsed around a lot, but OK, big problems come later mostly. At the station everybody said bye then they left.

In city-there, I got no more house, see, no more family. The others, they went home: Haïssama went back to Einguela, Warya to District 5, Ayanleh to Balbala an all. An so, all the other guys left but hey, no problem. They said: we gonna get together in front of headquarters tomorrow, ask for demobilization money, OK? Aïdid an me, we were too mad after that. Without thinking we just went to Siesta beach, where there's French faggots—military looking for little kids. OK, first of all, us, we not kids; an then, we don't look like faggots; an then watch out, we got weapons. We told old war stories for fun. We smoked a lot too; we thought about cool nice job to make money. We thought too much. We flipped out. Aïdid, he wanted to be smuggler in Loyada (that, border with Somaliland. Somaliland, maybe you don't know it yet, that OK, it not known like me Binladen, is all). Then, I said stop to Aïdid, we not gonna put demobilize money into this business-there, that too dumb. Me, I said we gonna go party well-well, then we gonna look for vitaminized job without paying a franc. Aïdid he OK-OK with that but hey, he don't know my secret yet, right? He said, how we gonna find vitaminized job? So I played boss. I yelled real-real loud: let's smoke first; after that, I give you solution. I was assawayed, scuse me, I'm out of it a little. Hahahaha, Assoweh I almost said like an ass, Assoweh that my old name cause now my name Binladen, the terriblific boss. Wait, don't make strategic mistake (that true military language) right away even if Aïdid a brother, right? So I said like that, gotta use survival technique, tomorrow or day after we see bout finding vitaminized job. Aïdid, he didn't have mistrust. An me, I didn't play my last card. Not so dumb, Binladen, right?

30

ABDO-JULIEN

FALL 1892. They were exhibiting Ka'lina Amerindians from French Guyana completely naked in a Parisian park at the same time as our grandfathers in traditional dress, gathered in a flimsy hut indicating their generic name—Somalis—in the Zoological Garden of Acclimation. Take the Chemins de fer de l'Ouest, the Western Railroad, and get off at Porte Maillot station, said the poster announcing the attraction in all the French newspapers. All that memory is available with one little click. Thanks, Internet. To think that Grandpa served as a soldier whose assignment was to watch the borders for the Republic that had put his grandfather in a cage of a zoo open to the winds. And what do I have to with all this? Now that I think about it, I'm closely connected to that past, that colonial memory not always the color of the pink panther. That's why I sometimes reject that shared memory, and at the same time reject myself, reject my maternal side and my skin, which in fact isn't all that light. Repress my whole being, express myself loudly too, and shout from the rooftops: "Do not call me a mulatto, a *métis*. Metis was the first wife of Zeus, king of the Olympian gods. She died horribly." But people here don't know that, either. So? So, don't breathe a word of it.

31

ALICE

IF YOUR BODY germinates and swells, if your heart pounds like the surf, what could be more normal? I push the rumpled sheet away with my hand; I crush the doubt that assails me under my heel. I seek in vain the heat of his body. I can sense his smell floating through the room; I still have the taste of his sweat in my mouth. I resonate with him with every fiber in my body; my skin spontaneously catches fire at his contact. I curl up with love inside his arms. Hold your breath; repeat without opening your mouth "I'm so happy!" Suddenly I can see the world with the eyes of the heart. Every second is an eternity; I flame with a joy I cannot hide. My head is resting on his lower belly, which goes up and down with the rhythm of his peaceful breathing. The two tips of my breasts are delightfully compressed by his shins. With one hand, I stroke the light moss of his ebony hairs, watching the dark honey of his eyes from the corner of mine. With the other hand, I stroke my sex wet and hot as burning spices. I hold my breath to prolong the exquisite moment.

A metallic sound attracts my attention. It's coming from the outside, from the street perhaps. Really, I have a hard time believing that right now he may be at police headquarters in a tiny room reeking of the urine from a whole gang of delinquents, the vomit of drunks, and the blood of the poor crucified people relegated to the basement. And all that because of a goddamn petition asking for peace and the official recognition of the martyr Mahmoud Harbi. I spend my time running after his absence. I am going stark-raving mad, it couldn't be clearer. In the darkness of my memory, nothing comes knocking. I stroke the cold bed. No, he's right in front of me. He's coming out of the bathroom; he's modest, as usual. He lowers the shade of his eyes. His underpants are tight on him; I look at it insistently, detect an erection. My senses are fooling me; I'm imagining things. No, he is here, in front of me, his eyes fogged over by modesty. He's still astonished by my relaxed immodesty after all these years. Why is he hiding his virility with his right forearm? He slips in at my side; his hairless calf bumps my hip. I breathe in; I want his sex; I want it to find its way back into my humus, and roughly. I read somewhere that the female hyena has an erectile penis and even false testicles. As she's bigger than her mate and dominates him, it seems natural for her to possess the genital attributes of the so-called stronger sex, don't you think? Wait, I just found a hair finer than an eyelash in the bed, and it's black. It must be his; it's the only thing that connects me to him at this moment. I am hot and cold at the same time. I would like to be somewhere else—far away from here, in any case. To live through a night of love with him. The last one?

I can see myself back on a beach in Brittany; I'm fourteen. It's in Saint-Lunaire, to be exact. I am part of a group of adolescent girls in bathing suits. Young girls in bloom with their budding breasts, a spot of sweat under each armpit. All the grace of human clay. Men's eyes are concupiscent, and we drown our fear under an avalanche of giggles. It must be three or four in the afternoon. A sea breeze, an angry word or a ray of the sun, and a shiver runs through our skin, freezes us. Our bathing suits and bras shield from indiscreet glances the ripe fruit, ready to be weighed with a trembling hand. Danger is approaching; it's the silhouette of two men in the prime of life. A slight sensation of dizziness. They draw closer still, talking all the while. Suddenly we get up and run over to our parents, who have remained on the beach.

32

ABDO-JULIEN

AT THE CORNER OF Rue d'Athènes and Avenue Clémenceau, the café Chez Abdou is a favorite meeting place where the finest rumors are passed around, not like the flat old news you can find everywhere else. (Note that in this whole business section of the city, as in the rest of it, most streets are named after European cities, like Berne, Rome, Paris, or Berlin. What's really surprising is that no president ever changed them, in fact nobody refers to these ordinary names, streets without a name that word-of-mouth has baptized Café Street, Hindi Barber Street, the street of the Junkmen, etc.) The café is mainly a series of white plastic chairs under the arcades along the sidewalk. Only four of their columns are freshly painted: candy pink for the bottom, sky blue for the top. The customers are free to congregate there according to time of day, affinity, and habit. There they drink very sweet tea with milk and, more rarely, suitably sweetened coffee in long Duralex glasses. You can detect a scent of something unfinished in the air, a certain provisory feeling, like the dream of a real city deferred.

There is no more entertainment like the movies used to be: the main theater, south of the city—Le Paris—was transformed many years ago into the headquarters of an austere, evangelical religious association. The very charismatic Sheikh Artawi and his virulent lieutenant preach there all day long. Fortunately, little open-air booths spring to life once evening has come. Nothing could be simpler; a few broken-down tables under a lamppost, and a whole crowd of people come swarming around the domino players. A more serious clientele of minor civil servants comes to Abdou's to feel the temperature of the city, and a swarm of plainclothes policemen and informers of all kinds slip in among them more easily than a hammerhead shark in the midst of a school of mackerel. Papa doesn't set foot there any more; the petition probably has something to do with that.

Recently, rumors have been going around about the new exterminating angel, the darling of the rabble, Osama bin Laden himself. It seems the authorities are very concerned about the explosion of slogans and graffiti singing the glories and inevitable victory of the Great Bearded One: a gigantic "Long Live Osama" has been scrawled over the wall at the entrance to the public high school for almost three days now. T-shirts bearing his face are proudly exhibited on Place Rimbaud or Place Menelik. Other slogans painted on the walls of the city have been reported, other words of aggressive sympathy in strategic points of the capital. The French military—and more recently the Americans and Germans—will not fail to classify, photograph, and carefully analyze every atom of the wall thus profaned before sending it off to Washington or Berlin for a series of complementary examinations. Battalions of Marines and the soldiers of the Bundeswehr are, in fact, looking for the elusive man of the caves. Would the hyena emerge from the bed of the dried-out wadi, from the belly of the protecting cactus? Every evocation of his name is submerged by a sea of rumors and terrified faces. Reports from some editorialists in New York, on the strength of statements from Pentagon officials, have located him in the nakedness of nearby Somalia. Which more than one native of the country has found astonishing, although they are usually placid and not very impressionable.

During the last presidential elections, the first in the era of the multiparty system, I accompanied Papa early in the morning. There were already a lot of people in front of the polling place. Plainclothes policemen, security agents in their little black cars, easy to spot from far away. A dozen uniformed policemen had the voters stand in two parallel lines and then ushered them into the voting place, normally just an elementary school. There was a lot of electricity in the air, for the neighborhood is known to be openly favorable to the opposition, like all the neighborhoods of the *magalla*. Informers were pacing back and forth in the schoolyard near the fountain that ordinarily attracts the games and laughter of the students. Policemen gave us scalding looks when we reached the threshold of the voting place. Others were seeing old ladies to the door; they were holding their newly stamped voting card in one hand and a thousand-franc bill in the other, the spoonful of honey after the bitter pill.

33

AWALEH

WHAT CAN ONE SAY about the multitude of djinns that surround us throughout our lives, of the band of frowning demons with heavily wrinkled brows who keep watch on our slightest feelings and impulses, and the trolls throwing us into the depths of disgrace at the first mistake? What can one say about those invisible beings who have one foot in the realm of the visible? What can we make of those nymphs who set monstrous traps for us, capitalizing on our little weaknesses, our occasional blindness; they lure us with fantasies like bathing the body of our lovers in the reflections of the moon, probing everywhere and seeking what can be said in what is impossible to say. How can we avoid awakening the spirits who hibernate in the bottom of our own darkness? Man is a wheezing, crotchety mollusk, dragging himself along on the thread of his fate. He dreams his life on a large scale but that can't be. He is there, terribly anxious; daily effort has chipped away at him, and he has settled into a convenient silence. The worst is yet to come. If happiness existed in this world here below, it would take the shape of a fountain of milk, the Ancients thought. God would be maternal, would breast-feed the little birds, the little refugees, the malnourished, the orphans, everything life drops and abandons by the roadside. As I think of Him, I immediately open myself to Him, to pray serenely. To chant, with my eyes closed in ecstasy, the ninety-nine names of the very holy Prophet. That is how I regain peace of mind and body.

What will tomorrow bring? No one can dare to say. No sign on the open palm, no prophetic calligraphy on the hand of Fatima. We always think at first that all we undertake will last our whole life long, and then we have to face up to the obvious: that's absolutely not the way it is. So we lose ourselves in conjectures. Will babies get their mothers' milk again, suckled at the breast, and not that revolting powder, white as aloe juice, given out by the UNDP,[1] the WFO,[2] the UNHCR,[3] or some other charitable agency—the milk we call "refugee milk" since this milk arrived in Year One of Independence? It came at the same time as our relatives driven from Ethiopia or Somalia by the war between the Somalis and the Ethiopians, two age-old enemies in the Horn of Africa, according to commentators foreign to the region. Let us wager that this will always be the ordinary course of things. There are two kinds of children: the children of Nido, nourished with powdered milk normally and legally imported, the most numerous—not always sons and daughters of refugees, since three-fifths of the country's children survive on that miraculous powder and thus depend on a pittance from humanitarian aid—and the other children. There are two kinds of fathers: those who give themselves over to the rite of the purple stem they are forever chewing, that khat which is exported all the way to Vancouver these days, and the others, who would like to have this luxury but do not have

1. United Nations Development Programme.—*Author's note*
2. World Food Organization.—*Author's note*
3. United Nations High Commission for Refugees.—*Author's note*

the means. Those who keep hanging onto khat like the swarm on the bough are plugged into the ten thousand watts of the rumbling snores of Radio *Mabraze.** And so? Well, nothing. *Hak,* nada, zilch, *niente.* Mamas sit rolling the beads of their rosary, sing songs of longing for the milk warm from the udders of the camel, chat of legends from an earlier time and country in honor of the trucks that bring bags of flour, powdered milk, sugar, durum wheat, brown soap, and cans of oil. The trucks and their drivers are adorned with the attributes formerly given to nomadic heroes wild with warlike furor, to Bedouins, wielders of the cutlass. Some of them show teary faces every time a convoy leaves, wondering when a compassionate God will make them return. The sooner the better, groan the standing ones with their stunted faces, the rubbish-dealers of hope. Tomorrow *inshallah mubarakh,* by the grace of the very holy sheikh Abdelkader Djilani, add the seated ones. A ballet of glances rises to heaven. The ones lying down say nothing. Decidedly, those trucks are the saviors of the world. They drive away in a line, leaving behind them clouds of kerosene mingled with dust. Plastic bags spin like tops all along the cracked trail. The sky that dries everything out, dirty and gray like the collar of a shirt that has been worn on a very hot day, keeps coming through between the swirls of dust. The thirty-two teeth of famine grind in silence. Tree shoots that will never come up are dreaming of leaves, of vigorous roots, proliferating rhizomes, young downy shoots, tangled brambles, blackish little roots and fragile seeds, impetuous and triumphant. What will tomorrow bring? Luck, we're waiting for luck, we're waiting for luck we're telling you, for a godsend, providence, *baraka,* luck, see? Some eat up their little bit of hope in the shade of an acacia tree. Children pick up grain after grain, at the exact spot where the trucks were parked, a little fistful of corn or rice. They have one foot in life, the other in nothingness. And yet, it's the finest day of the season in the village of As-Eyla, transformed into a "camp for displaced persons" as the national press decorously puts it. The rest of the time they remain lying on their mat, so weak and asthenic, curled in the fetal position, their big dry eyes staring at the horizon line. What could they possibly be staring at? Their bloodless pupils wander from bald hill to bald hill. Only desert mirages take off from those runways, as nomadic pride is a thing of the past. ("Never will I submit to a life where the belly guides the eyes," they used to swear in times gone by. May God seal their eyes and let them sleep the sleep of the just!) Fat flies swallowing tiny insects and ants stampeding as if struck by lightning have a crush on them. The toothy jaws of the dragon of death grind up the sickly brotherhood. One or two cats, their skeleton showing beneath their graying coat, their stringy fur longer than the mustache of Mephistopheles, stand guard with lonely hearts. They, too, do not like to meow, don't like the noises of others, humans or animals. It is in silence, under the stingy shade of an acacia or a ficus, that they find peace in the world. Hours add onto hours to give birth to days exactly the same as the other days. Thus, smoothly and quietly, unfolds the odyssey of a life 360 degrees open to the pre-desert. The lightness of a smile should not push into the background all the bitterness of the difficult job of living, with its duties and torments, its feeling of thickness and complexity, its flint rubbed until it sparks. The vanity of things has evaporated all by itself like the languages we call dead. To predict is heresy; tomorrow is entirely veiled by the will of the Majestic One. We must try to live our lives as seriously as children play their games, while knowing that cops and robbers are only roles and postures to be played with the greatest seriousness. You've got to smile, too. Even in your death throes you must hold back your drool; that is what a saying still in use today tells us.

34

BASHIR BINLADEN

WE WERE TOGETHER every single minute, Aïdid an me. Us two, we more than partners, we true brothers same ball same goal. Aïdid said he gonna find me a pretty AK-47 for present, day I get married. You bet! there no weapon shortage, he swore like that down on one knee, his eyes shining strong like me when I'm high. By the Good Lord who salted the sea you gotta believe me, Aïdid added. OK, don't go all upset, I believe you, I said. Now, life hard, real shameful even. We out of the game cause we got no more uniform, no more Kalash to panic people on the street, no more food to gobble. Gotta hustle well-well now an later. So we go to Ethiopian girls' bars, where French military they go drink beer an grope ass of *nayas.** We say hi to everybody. We go see French soldiers; say something in their ear. After that, we stand attention front of French military cars. When French soldiers leave for bed or go to more bars to drink some more, us, we pick up the change. If they don't pay, watch out, danger of death for their tires, right? Job-there, it specially weekend cause French or German soldiers (those guys, little greenhorns don't really know the rules how you get along), they don't go out every night. No, they too scared cause of Gulf War,

Iraq War, Somalia War, an terriblific bomb attacks. Terrorists, they no good for morale an no good for business, Moussa he told me that too.

Moussa he was taxi driver before always making travel. So weekends are good-good for hustle cause goverment got no money. Goverment employees, they been waiting for salary fourteen months. Now, it serious economic crisis, believe me faithfully. When you ask for money, the other guy always answer the same sentence like parrot too-too old: inshallah tomorrow, the Good Lord who salted the sea will not forget us, his children. So now, I get real mad. I do my boss number an I yell: you fat motherfucka, gimme the money right away. An then, Aïdid he come up behind like fast fullback of Real Madrid Roberto Carlos an he bazook the other guy's head. Can't waste bullet cause we got no more khakis an we don't eat army chow no more. Club on the other guy's head, that's enough. After, we go pick up the change an girls not too ugly. We smoke, we drill the girls' asses, we smoke, we drill the girls' asses, like that till the sun rise over Stinksea (that, neighborhood of wild tough-guys like us *shiftas** or the *kapos, kefkefs,* pimps, an the other guys). Every morning the sea carries in corpses fat as Hindi cows (that I know for sure cause of Hindi movies in Al Hilal movie house). OK, none of my business. Those dead guys not always wild hoods, see. They even important genlemen in suit-an-tie: teacher, doctor, union guy an all. Secret police, they suicide a lot-lot, an then they throw corpses into our neighborhood. That way City say yes gotta kill all the hoods or lock em up like the asshole general who screwed up coup. Life like that, one day you pick up money, next day you lose your life. There even babies who scream for two hours an then they quick-quick gone (they called *shafeec,* in other words they went back inside mama's belly). His mama left behind like bundle of dirty laundry; she cries a lot-lot. Life like that.

Yesterday we pitched our tent on Stinksea beach, true, tent a little dirty, but the not-ugly girls who smoke with Aïdid an me, they love it. An then, the other wild hoods an the *shiftas*, they know right away we still military without fear an pity like Janaleh, the dry lawman (that his nickname) who comes to drink beer with us. Janaleh he laughing all the time cause in his pocket-there he got a big stock of pink pills (Excedrin, melatonin, Valium, Vicodin . . . label say that). Janaleh real wild. Everything he don't sell, it for him. Life always like that. Some people laugh; others cry like mamas without babies. Others nervous like a khat-grazer with no khat.

35

ALICE

WHEN A WIFE IS CROSS with her husband or neglected by him, she goes back to her father's household and can't come back unless she's accompanied by a delegation that includes the members of his family laden with gifts. Before that, the husband has been summoned, sermonized, and returned to the straight and narrow if need be. A ram is slaughtered and the quarrel drowned in the family celebration. If, for one reason or another, the wife is not brought back at the end of a few days, she is considered divorced from her husband. At least, that's how things went in the time when the importance of a family was calculated more by the number of its neighbors than by the size of its flock. In the same way, one did not marry inside the clan but allied oneself with another clan from the great tribal family. Today, it's all going to the devil, he mumbles.

That just shows that my father-in-law has remained the only member of the family I enjoy seeing again. When he has nothing personal to tell me, he instructs me in the customs of the country; it's his way of breaking the ice and being useful.

"My dear Alice, you can't imagine how clever our Bedouins are, the very ones those travelers or researchers of yours describe as ignorant. Believe it or not, when a baby camel happened to die, it was immediately replaced by a straw dummy so that the mother would continue to give milk. The same technique was used for a cow deprived of her calf. The dummy was made from the hide of the dead baby camel stuffed with straw; it was disposed of after five months, which is how long lactation lasts. Ingenious, isn't it? But—for there is always a but with human activities—the dummy had no effect on the she-goat and the ewe."

I can sense that he hasn't come just to teach me these inert things marinating in oblivion. He hovers around me; I leave him to his little game, and this man, whose shreds of words are usually so parsimonious at this time of day, turns into my confidant. He knows that words spoken in a confidential tone have more impact than words proclaimed loud and clear. I throw him a line: you've never told me the meaning of your name Awaleh. "Oh, that means 'the lucky one' or more precisely 'He will live'; at times of great pandemics or famines it was given to newborn babies to ward off fate. You know, Alice, your six-month-old son and thus my grandson, by the grace of the Majestic One, you know that he was born on the night of destiny, the night of Miraj, *al leyl'al miraj* as Muslims say the world over." And what does that imply—destiny? I stammer, trying to look natural. "Your husband told you nothing about this? That doesn't surprise me at all; that's the way he is—too westernized; I can see how far the son has moved away from his father. Other days, other ways. Luckily I'm here to connect the threads of spiritual and temporal things, the visible and the invisible, my dear Alice. Miraj is the night of the ascent to heaven of our prophet Mohammed, may his name be praised to all eternity! who reached the spiritual world of celestial Jerusalem by riding the winged horse Bouraq, led by the angel Djibril. The steed of the Prophet—may his name be praised by all tiny creatures like us!—was described by the chroniclers as an animal having wings on his thighs pushing his legs forward so hard he could attain the speed of light."

What is going to happen to my baby? I say, holding back a tear. "Nothing but good; all mothers pray to deliver their children from evil on the night of destiny. Your baby is blessed, blessed three times over. We're lucky, you know? A baby like this one at the first try, bravo, girl!"

I wanted to point out that my baby was also just as old as Independence (independence is above all the power of utopia— it is all the battles dreamt and fought, and their catastrophic future)—but he had already turned away. He left as surreptitiously as he had come.

36

BASHIR BINLADEN

THE GOVERMENT STILL got no money. So I say we gotta start vitaminized job tomorrow. I woke up Aïdid; he was too-too floppy cause of the pills Janaleh gave out. We set up front of American embassy. Lot of poor jerks there with blankets lying down on sidewalks all the way up to the École de la Nativité. Then, we kick an punch everybody an take up position two yards away from the gate. But they still there, some of em snoring loud like inside their mama's belly. Some of em look like they already in the grave. We stamp our feet; c'mon get out of there, we here to work. We brought empty folders an files to look serious. Course we also brought our little weapons like Yemenite knives, box cutters an all for dissuasion (that military language, very correct even). After, we smoked, but real-real Camel cigarettes with camel on the pack. We like Camels cause of camel, cause that, animal of nomads, right? When sun began to get too hot, we saw lot of people coming in by bus, by taxi, an even on foot, the ones who're broke. An even good-looking girls who got lot-lot of nice perfume psst! psst! on the neck an arms. Their perfume, it smell good from French Consulate to far-far away Aïdid said, cause don't forget, real vitaminized job is tomorrow front of French Consulate. One day it cowboy embassy, another day blue-white-an-red consulate. That way everybody happy. An then, blue-white-an-red consulate also give visa for Belgium, Holland, Sweden, etc. My idea-there real good, don't you think? Hey, that was my secret, got it now, you smarties out there? That way, people don't send out to look for us saying: where they go, those two hoods without pity?

So, one day it this way, next day that way. Friday rest, weekend here at home cause everything closed. Ah! two customers walking up to me with fresh face an toothpaste smile like commercials on DRT (that, Radio TV in our country, you didn't forget that, right?). The two customers, one pay one thousand francs, other pay one thousand francs. They don't cause no problems or else watch out. Anyways, they real happy. They sneak in the line-there center-forward an they think they gonna get visa for New York or Washimton right away. My job, real classy cause number one, it real easy job: you push away the little weak guys, you get in center-forward position in the long-long line, an after that you give your place to the customer who pay right away, an number two, cause there many-many customers; everybody wanna leave this shitty country. Everybody, they yell: I got a brother in Paris, I got uncle in America, I want a job in Australia, I got refugee family in Canada. Visa, money-transfer, certificate, consulate . . . It ten past ten, job over for today. But hey, it not illegal to pick up money somewhere else. Lessee if there French or German soldiers in town, to scrounge money. Visa, transfer, consular, tralala . . . Visa, transfer, tralala . . .

37

ABDO-JULIEN

THE PRESIDENT, the second of that name, His Excellency El Hadji Abdoulwahid Egueh, was elected rather democratically, if we are to believe the foreign observers sent by the OAU, the Conseil de la Francophonie, and the UN. Eight experienced emissaries followed the election, in which His Excellency received over 60 percent of the vote. The main leader of the opposition got close to 26 percent. Two other parties of the disunited opposition—puppet parties, in the eyes of public opinion—shared the crumbs. The whole business was buckled up in two or three sighs, His Excellency immediately congratulated by France, the monarchies of the Persian Gulf, and finally by the rest of the international community. All the representatives of said community congratulated themselves on the return of peace and the success of the demobilization process, which returned some sixteen thousand people to civil life with the help of the UNDP and various NGOs. Not forgetting the patent failure of the coup d'état that ended, fortunately, without too much bloodshed. There were a few protests here and there, but nothing to alarm the emissaries' conscience, which a few displayed without excessive exertion. More than the election of the president—quite predictable, after all—what still affects people is the "patriotic contribution": up to a fourth of one's salary deducted at the source, even well after hostilities ended.

38

ALICE

I TOUCH MYSELF; I delicately stroke the brushy tuft, the pink of my moist flesh slightly sticky, light mixing with dark. A peony. The invisible stirring is there, right next to me, a subterranean heating of my body. I feel him tight against me. I can feel him even if he's still rotting in the central police station. I'm feeling him more than ever. I slip two fingers inside the moving, half-open silk, moist and pearly, smiling to the stars. I can see my man standing behind me again, his body glued to mine, his body cutting a narrow path between desire and memories, his hands weighing my breasts. I sigh, purr like a well-fed cat. He turns me over, sucks my nipples. I'm drowning. Got to hold myself back and take a deep breath, the little voice inside me says without desire or displeasure. He catches hold of me again, lifts me up, sets me delicately on the bed, holding me by the hips. I lose myself in his arms; his lips run down my spine. He's getting ready to stick his turgescence into the very depths of my flesh. A deep song rises from the earth, floods the skies. His blood is beating and beating in his temples, in his jugular veins, his breast, his forearms. My man crushing me with his full weight, bringing back my knees before he opens them to

set, no, to plant his trunk between them and move inside them
up and down, up and down, his two legs completely parallel and
even squeezed together, the rectangle of his back compressing
and relaxing as the breath goes in and out of his chest clinging
to mine, his arms now slipped beneath the shade of my armpits.
I can feel my wetness swelling until it bursts.

39

BASHIR BINLADEN

I'M DEAD, I'm almost dead. You think that a bunch of lies, well then me, Binladen, I'm gonna tell you everything. Demobilization money never got into our hands. Right away I knew it was too rotten, that business-there. Government said I don't wanna pay nothing, don't have a franc in the till. Us, we got the message, we attacked headquarters not too-too hard, just to scare, to get the money, see. The president, he don't find this funny, chiefsa staff neither. They went an brought tanks right away from military camp Sheikh-Osman an even from Nagadh military training center. And no warning bang-bang-bang they fire at everybody. Like the last time on the demobilized with no legs no arms an no money. Lot of people killed on the spot not just demobilized, like my good buddy Aïdid (may his soul rest in peace, *Allah arhamu,** an vengeance some day I swear it). Even old civilians, handicapped, retired, old mamas who sell cigarettes on street-there, they shelled everybody. Operation Dead Town. Worse than the other asshole's screwed-up coup. I swear to God, me, Binladen the terriblific, my body move all by itself cause of great fear-there. All the people alive—not that many, really—they were running all over. I dunno how I

got back to the neighborhood of ambassadors. I saw the scared
people an I follow, that's all. This time you've had it, I told myself; it's the end of my poor little life that's all, everybody gotta
right to die some day, right, even Binladen, so what?

   I say that to myself when I saw thousands of police in front
of embassies. Then, I dunno why, I found myself inside French
consulate with four other men. I think I fell into coma, OK not
big coma, no, little coma for a couple minutes or a few hours,
little coma like goalie KO cause his head hit the goalpost hard
an then stretcher an substitution. So, I was in little coma cause
something hit my head-there. Little coma, still danger a little.
OK, so there I am in front of ambassador of France, the fat genleman in shirt with red-white-an-blue flowers, you didn't forget,
did you? Ambassador, today he wearing white shirt an red tie
like the blood of sheep with throat slit for Aïd feast. Ouch ouch
my head-there, it hurt too much. Wire snapped inside or what?
So, the four men, they argue loud with ambassador. I didn't
understand everything in their big an rich French. Cept a genleman was saying: he can't escape in that crazy city with those
drugged policemen and all. The ambassador, he answered: I
don't give a shit about that mess, then he calmed down a little,
but the man didn't let it drop. Then, another man said: France
has to protect him with his son, an there he pointed to me with
his intellectual's finger, clean an all. Yes, his nice wife killed by
the soldiers an drugged policemen was French, so they must
begin investigation right away, must send him right away to
France with his son, an there he points to me, Binladen the terriblific now sort of broken. Me, I don't have the strength to open
my mouth. I look an look an I don't say nothing. Ambassador,
he said: OK your wife she's French but she lived with you; she
never came by to say hello at the embassy even on July 14, the
national holiday. She took too many risks; there's nothing I can
do, you understand. The intellectual genleman he got real-real

mad, he hit bang on the flowerpots like enraged striker going for goal. Outside we could hear bullets and bombs whistling an singing a lot. The argument with ambassador, it lasted all afternoon. Then, the ambassador left to take care of his black dog. The four men, they go crazy like Italian fans who lost World Cup final. Me, Binladen, I got a head-there heavy like military truck; I watch everything an I don't say nothing. Almost night now. We slept like that outside on the ground in the courtyard, each one in his corner like little scared dog. We didn't swallow nothing but cigarette smoke to drive away fear.

Next morning the ambassador came back with another shirt but same tie. He said like a boss to the three other men: you, you can leave, I have received assurance from the authorities. The others, they didn't stand up; they were too KO. Then, it our turn. You and your son, I can at a *pinch*—he repeated that pinch-there three times—get you on tonight's flight. I'm going to sign a permit for urgent repatriation; you'll try to handle your administrative formalities once you're in Paris. No residency visa; don't count on it. That's all I can do for you. As for the investigation, that will wait until your country regains its sanity. And he left without saying good-bye.

EPILOGUE

To tell is suffering. To be silent is suffering, too.
—AESCHYLUS

HARBI

TODAY, EXILE is making eyes at everybody: individuals young and old, entire families, and whole regions have thrown themselves onto the roads with their pockets full of hope and fear spurring them on. They go wherever the wind may take them, with filth and rotting corpses for company. They get lost in the labyrinth of bad luck, and hurricanes fling them deep into dungeons, into the dark pit of ordeals, and even into countries they never heard of in their former lives, like Finland, Iceland, or Alaska. These are people who have often forgotten their age and changed names many times; their inner clock stopped the day they left. Their brains took flight before their muscles; they have wandered from a makeshift shelter to an airlock the color of night. Borders, oceans, laws, and police cannot stem this human flood. And even the shaved heads of old, worried Europe, the neo-Nazi torchbearers, the arsonists of shelters for stateless foreigners can do nothing to contain them. And here they are, my brothers in misfortune, dazed and frightened in the cold climate, terrified by the administrative mess inherent in the European paradise, my brothers discovering some legal refinement their colonial education had never touched on, like in Switzerland. They had left their not-so-ancient cities to find themselves stuck between un-Christian charity, liberal Jesuitism, Protestant deceit, and Helvetic slyness, not to mention the devious lacework made in Strasbourg and Brussels. Nothing to destroy our timid hopes—the hopes of the humble—nothing to scar our dreams: asylum is the azure sky, the fertile horizon. It's the end of hunger that hollows the cheeks and makes the eyes flare. Dryness to the bone. Watch out, you're falling into cheap lyricism, whispers a little mocking voice inside me. No need to be a doctor to see that our thinness isn't fake. Nothing to do with the false paleness of models with the buttocks and thighs of a grasshopper, or the health of an outdoor daredevil, or the thin frame of the workers of the high seas, the walnut tan of soldiers of the Alpine summits, the raging hunger of the mountain specialists of the Tour de France, the energy of cycling road-eaters and the hollowed-out torso of Sunday Poulidors.[1] That's the swaggering stuff spread all over the newspapers I pick up off the low tables and seats in Roissy.

As for us, we describe ourselves as present absentees, weak-kneed nobodies who have lots of things to say about their previous life, but the traffic jam of words in our throats makes us more silent than a regiment of Buddhist monks. We remain prisoners of the river of words that flow on in meanders: in what language should we light the fire of confession? What we could tell you would surely make you lose all taste for sleep and the desire to grow fat from idleness at home. What we could tell you would appeal as much to your heart as to your conscience. Deaf-mutes now, we drag around our diminished silhouettes in silence, so lost in solitude that we can't talk any more and no longer know how. We are grains of sand washed up onto

1. Raymond Poulidor was a great French cyclist.—*Translators' note*

someone else's desert, and that's what we'll always remain. No one running after us and no sign of hospitality in sight. We no longer even have the mats we would sleep on once the little loincloth separating the children's corner from the parents' was lowered. We've left our stories, our melodies, our books of magic, and our ancestors behind. The danger awaiting us is this: if you live only in the present, you're likely to be buried with the present.

I'll remember for a long time that group of refugees storming a commercial plane in Ambouli airport. Like a swarm of locusts, they cluster together in the middle of the tarmac, then, on a sign one of them gives from who knows where, they rush up the gangway. Girls in hijabs, middle-aged women in chadors leaving a long trail of heady perfume behind them, boys in ill-matched suits, mothers hobbled by tight dresses, patriarchs lost in the jumble of orders and counter-orders. The neat-looking female flight attendants are completely at a loss. Their definitive gestures and their suddenly authoritarian tones are signs of impotence. No sooner are they seated than the new arrivals get up, block the aisles, come back to sit down, get up again. Order and measure are sent off reeling; they change places, change seats. They transfer an uncle with a bad headache to the other end of the Airbus. They call out to a sister, a cousin, a neighbor they think they recognize. They complain aloud and have absolutely no clue how uncomfortable the people around them feel, nor do they see the dark looks sent their way since they've arrived. The European passengers who boarded the plane at Saint-Denis de la Réunion hunch down in their seats and let the storm pass. But *they* don't notice. They come from Mombasa; they fled Mogadishu. They might have been Tamils, Sudanese, Afghans, Kurds, Albanians, or Bosnians. They are the millions of humans with a number from the United Nations High Commission for Refugees and a rationing card. They are the peoples in motion through the shrinking world.

Who will extend their hospitality to us like lovely Calypso, who put her milky arms around an Odysseus in rags? Who will protect us as the eyelid protects the eye? Many of us just hope to get into a shelter, a humanitarian emergency reception center—oh yes, that's what they're called. To cross the tunnel under the Channel, with our family if at all possible, with or without the agreement of the men who offer to make the crossing easier—for money—in order to find ourselves in England without being able to stammer a *yes* or a *no thank you*. The first natives of the country we glimpsed at the airport counter were already frowning with animosity. Our last fantasies dissolved. All we could see of them was their closed faces and the accusing hooked index finger. I hear that special words are traveling from group to group, transit from mouth to mouth. England, which was only a word like any other, a fantasy like any other, a distant echo of that longed-for Eldorado, is stirring in every mouth. That word is about to become an open-sesame, a common fate. I remember now that João, an Angolan intellectual I met in the airport, was loudly repeating the credo and chorus of the national anthems of big countries. He certainly was shouting his head off, belching out an unrecognizable mixture in every direction: "*Libertade o morte . . . Deutschland, Deutschland über alles . . . God save the Queen . . . In God we trust . . . True North strong and proud . . . Allonz'enfants de la patrieee . . .*"

Wait. Still a few more days, a few more weeks. Maybe a few months, adds the small voice, casually pointing out to me that my own little exile is nothing compared to the crossing of the Red Sea by the sons of Moses over five thousand years ago. Tormented by sleep, we turn over in our mouths, again and again, what happened yesterday and the day before; human

memory is an eternal support that enables what usually with-
ers away, forgotten and lost in the limbo of the present, to come
back to life. Nothing has gotten any clearer except the renewed
mystery of waiting; our existence is a one-eyed amphibious ka-
leidoscope. I must get slick enough to go through walls, as my
new condition demands. To survive melancholy and thumb my
nose at emptiness, from time to time I reread my virtual travel
journal, which is necessarily cerebral. It's a jumble of dog-eared
pages, childish scribbling (I've even kept some drawings Abdo-
Julien made when he was around six, a bookmark in the book
of memory), bay leaves, cactus and aloes flowers stuck to the
covers, family photos, and many other trivial objects, like that
seashell I picked up one day on White Sand Beach in Tadjoura.
I hang on to this wavering, inaudible, invisible next-to-nothing,
already vanished. To forget for a moment the Arctic men with
no sense of humor who will eventually take down our sworn
statements. And read, keep reading. Do not break down; do not
cry in front of the whole world. At any rate, my culture does
not predispose me to cry. Especially not a man—and what's
more, an ex-father. Hold back my tears, and read, read, read.
Keep reading, in every situation, everywhere. Read the way
other people count sheep before going to sleep. I can see myself
again confined in the little room of the central police station. I
concentrate on all the sounds around me. Very quickly, I was
pushing away the shouts, the blows, the crying, and the snores.
I trained my ear to capture the slightest sounds in the distance.
And that miraculous bit of fishing saved me from depression.
I had found the only pleasant way of animating the scene: lis-
tening to the monotonous cooing of the pigeons. Their hoarse
song, repeated like a drunkard's speech, came to me rhythmi-
cally and took me out of the condition I was in. Luckily a bird
would fly off from time to time, flapping its wings as if to bring
oxygen to my ears and my mind. That's how I held out for weeks

and months. I had learned the ABCs of my new state: silence, exile, and cunning.

Avoid talking, talking too much; avoid attracting attention, like poor Ahmed Chehem, who died choked by his own chatter, his own words tumbling down his throat like so many stones carried away by the force of the torrent. He had a voice that did not come from the throat but from further away, from deeper, from the depths of his gullet; you might have thought he had a radio transmitter hidden deep inside his belly, mixed in with his sticky guts, set into the slime of intestinal vegetation. A broken voice, silenced for centuries and centuries. The sounds, the words, the ideas that came out of his mouth were from the other end of the world. They spoke of the exile of the sun, the terrors that men feel at the threshold of day. A jumble of dreams that hardly brush ordinary people's minds. Ahmed Chehem, who died just before the land of milk and honey of his dreams, after surviving the worst tortures of the thugs of President Egueh. Poor man! May God have mercy on his soul. *Allah arhamu!*

In between two silent readings, uncertainty. Why did everything happen so fast? Impossible to recapitulate the very last steps in one's fall. True, there was a yesterday full of both sun and fog, a "before" that I wouldn't renounce for anything in the world, and a present, right here, whose blurry progression is something like a snail's. The future is not obligatory; tomorrow we'll see about the future, *inshallah*. Waiting, still. Here we are, about to be propelled into serious cities, their dark alleys, their gray, aggressive winters, their reception centers with cold corridors and stingy lighting, their jails with their sterile silence. Smelling of cat piss forever. A veritable Biafra of the mind and feelings. Here, the afternoons are very short. The days seem to go by dressed in a thick coat, buttoned up to the collar. And we're the lucky ones: some of our brothers are in the far north, caught in the trap of howling blizzards and banners of ice hanging from the lampposts.

Exhausted, we were like the fog trying to cross an ocean. Our lives were spinning, sucked up in the eye of an enormous cyclone, and wouldn't stop spinning and spinning. We would plug up our ears so as not to hear the creaking of our bones, the whistling of our bowels, the air holes in our hearts. A crater would suddenly gobble us into its wide-open mouth. That was our recurrent dream.

We hear that the personnel managing the reception centers of the Red Cross and the Secours Populaire[2] avoid all contact with us. Can you believe it, they wash us from a distance with a hose. Aseptic masks protect their faces and rubber gloves their hands as they pass us a little splinter of soap, as if we were cankered with mold and covered with mange. The boldest of us walk out of the retention center in the night and find themselves in disaffected squats next to some railroad station or port, before the city files an eviction notice with the municipal authorities, and the zones around the trains and ports set up a heavy surveillance system with steel wire fencing and automatic doors. Every vehicle leaving these zones will be inspected from top to bottom by security guards equipped with thermal and carbonic gas detectors.

One night (or was it in broad daylight?) we left the country that existed so deeply inside us, saving what we still had—that is, our own carcass. We smelled of the grave from the outset. A country where life and death are churned in the same melting pot, where you go from eclipse to fall, your body frozen and your soul turned to stone. A country where rhythm has

---

2. Literally "People's Aid," a charitable NGO in France with Communist connections.—*Translators' note*

but two beats, and how sublime they are: warmth and humidity, light and shade, day and night. Like others, I had been a victim, according to the expression of a French journalist who was expelled as soon as he arrived, of the "coercion employed by the regime, which made sure it silenced all demands that went beyond its own sphere." And yet I had shown nothing but silence and patience before the noise of the world. A country where retracing one's tribal genealogy was becoming more and more pressing. A country where the avenues of the capital are covered with sewer water and give off an unbearable stench that the pumps of the sun are unable to evacuate. Here, all roads lead to the prefecture. We are now serving a suspended sentence on this earth, with no promise but humiliation at the end, in the company of all the other trash of the planet, at once victims, executioners, and witnesses. You need to leave in order to return and construct something; one can only build on ruins. That is how the cross-section of such an event must be depicted.

Roissy–Charles de Gaulle Airport. Five A M. Sky milky gray. Silence in the departure hall that has seen so many departures and returns, so many separations and reunions, so many absences and presences. Cargoes of exiles, theaters of cruelty and bitterness. Muffled steps in the halls, some rustling of silk or nylon. Tick-tack of the flight attendants' high-heeled shoes, quickening their pace. Tourists in shorts drag their flip-flops over the floor while the good Italian soles of businessmen in formal suits and closed faces slide along, powerful and assured in their progression. And there are a few of us, hunching into the bottom of our seats to get away from the viscous flow of the waves of travelers. The seats are midnight blue.

Thoughts are hammering at my temples, pounding against the walls of my skull like the backwash against a cliff. They escape in waves or in fragments. Ideas roaring in my ears;

thoughts ripened under the sun of my conscience, each more haunting than the last. They bear witness to a life crenellated with catastrophes. The only courageous act I ever did was to save a poor devil pushed around by the herd of human animals who killed my family and the whole country, too. Luckily for him, he was light enough to pass for my precious only child. A long, depressing day lies ahead of me. For a few moments, I can enjoy the calm and the silence.